Metaphorosis

February 2023

Beautifully made speculative fiction

Also from Metaphorosis

Metaphorosis Magazine

Metaphorosis: Best of 20xx
Metaphorosis 20xx: The Complete Stories
annual issues, from 2016

Monthly issues

Plant Based Press

Best Vegan Science Fiction & Fantasy
annual issues, 2016-2020

from B. Morris Allen:
Chambers of the Heart: speculative stories
Susurrus
Allenthology: Volume I
Tocsin: and other stories
Start with Stones: collected stories
Metaphorosis: a collection of stories

Verdage

Reading 5X5 x3: Changes
Reading 5X5 x2: Duets
Score – an SFF symphony
Reading 5X5: Readers' Edition
Reading 5X5: Writers' Edition

Vestige

The Nocturnals, by Mariah Montoya

Metaphorosis

February 2023

---

edited by
B. Morris Allen

ISSN: 2573-136X (online)
ISBN: 978-1-64076-251-0 (e-book)
ISBN: 978-1-64076-252-7 (paperback)

Metaphorosis
a magazine of speculative fiction
from
Metaphorosis Publishing

Neskowin

February 2023

The Excursionist of JCPenney

Chris Panatier

Lorraine sat in the passenger seat of the Buick with four flat tires, applying her usual shade of lipstick. The fact that the tires were flat was no bother; the car hadn't moved since her mother died twenty years before. Even if Lorraine could afford to get it running again, it wouldn't make any difference. She didn't know how to drive.

Doing her face in the Buick had been the routine going back to when mom would give her a lift to her job and she saw no reason to stop just because mom was dead. So, every morning at seven forty-five, she emerged from the senior living studio condominium that had been Mom's and was now hers, walked the fifteen steps to the petrified sedan, and eased herself into the passenger seat. Mom had been gone since Lorraine was forty-six, but their relationship remained complicated.

She imagined her mother sitting in the driver's seat, asking if Lorraine had her nametag and lunch—inquiries that Lorraine silently resented, because of course she did, she wasn't a child. Lorraine did miss the ride to work—the Florida summers were excruciating—but she didn't miss the condescension.

With her lips done, she dropped the stick into her purse. Mornings were the worst, when her brain wasn't yet occupied by work and was free to simmer about her life's many grievances. "I was smart," she declared, digging for the eyeliner. "As smart as Connie and way smarter than Mary." She took hold of the gear shift and wiggled it in frustration. "They were just pretty faces." If the family hadn't treated her like a helpless imbecile her whole life, then she might have built some independence. Even now, Mary had control of Lorraine's finances, which was a particularly sour twist of the knife.

She lined her left eye, then the right—the droopy one—as quickly as she could. Some mornings she just wanted to stab the pencil right through it. Better that people assumed she'd lost it to an accident, than make assumptions about her intelligence because of it. It barely worked anyway. The world was a jumble of color and shape through the bad eye, a kaleidoscope of fractured images that never quite made sense. The pieces always seemed to be drifting toward cohesion, but without ever actually arriving, the full picture just out of reach. Lorraine took it as a cruel taunt from the Universe. Sometimes, in angry bouts of spite, she would hold the eye open past the point when it seared, until her pain-addled mind composed mosaics of the broken pieces. Occasionally, the habit brought on strange glimpses of new places—faraway settings and locations that seemed real enough—but always distant and out of reach. Mostly, her eye just hurt.

Lorraine zipped her purse, checked her nametag, and stood from the car, grunting as she slammed the door. The sound might have been from the exertion or displeasure at her mother's memory. She supposed it was a dose of each.

Work didn't start for another hour and fifteen, but the walk took fifty minutes and she would need another ten or twenty to cool off once she arrived. She headed down the treeless road and around the pond rumored to have crocodiles or alligators—she could never remember the difference—and finally past the unoccupied guard station at the front of the community.

Turning down Greenwich Parkway, Lorraine mumbled her resentment. Her old familiar. She'd carried it with her since childhood, when people assumed she was inadequate because of the eye or her halting speech. She knew it wasn't the right way to live, spending so much of her energy detesting those who judged her. If only they'd given her a chance, she might have made friends. Might have cut the tethers that had kept her trapped. Might have seen the world.

But resentment was a loop, wasn't it? A vicious circle or whatever the term was. You decided to resent people even before they could judge you. And then they judged you anyway.

She pushed through the big glass doors to the store. This was the best part of her day, the move from sweltering heat to the frozen, artificial air. It was a transformation. Outside, she was an afterthought. But at JCPenney, she was important. *Essential.* She belonged. Part of a team that made the store go, all one hundred and forty-three thousand square feet of it. Lorraine knew every inch. So well, in fact, that her words didn't pile up if she had to tell a customer in Fine Jewelry how to get to the Home section. A senior member of the store, she could jump into any department, take inventory, fold blouses, even stock shelves if they didn't demand too high a reach. Her brain held a photo-perfect topographical map, with every product in its place. She could recite department, aisle, and shelf for over thirty-four thousand individual items, and had cold command of the on-line catalogue as well.

Roberta, the store supervisor, was sitting at one of the white tables in the break room, facing the tiny TV perched up in the corner. Roberta was the only employee with tenure over Lorraine, and had even hired her—which was a bit of a miracle, all things considered. Lorraine had managed to get in the door at a lot of places even though she only had high school, but the droopy eye and manner of talking had people cutting the interviews short.

It was Roberta who'd first offered her a job. She didn't seem to notice or care about her speech or her eye. In fact, Roberta's indifference to it made Lorraine want to tell her everything—like a strange reward for being decent. She wanted Roberta to know that her difficulties had no bearing on smarts, that she'd only made the mistake of getting near her father once while he was All The Way Drunk, and had walked away with a tongue that struggled with words and an eye that would never see the world the same way again. But beautiful Roberta didn't care about the eye. And Lorraine loved her for it.

"Hi, Roberta," said Lorraine, setting her bag onto the counter near the coffee machine. The pot hadn't been started and so she began the process. A filter from the cabinet, water from the sink, four level scoops from the tin. She snapped in the basket and hit the brew button, then turned to Roberta. "Roberta?"

"Headquarters sent out a list of store closures."

Lorraine didn't even register the words. They sounded like corporate speak and corporate speak was something Lorraine had learned to tune out. She let the phrase dissipate in the air and filled a mug with tap water, then sat across from her boss. "Did you see the hand truck of toasters sitting in the aisle between Baby and Women's?"

Roberta had her head down, face in hands. Lorraine twisted around and glanced at the television to see if there was bad news, but it was just a commercial for The Rug Guy. Turning back, she said, "Roy must have forgotten to bring them to the stockroom at the end of his shift last night. I can get them on the shelves before we open if there's space. I think—"

"Lorraine," said Roberta, looking up, eyes red and wet. "I had to fire Roy."

Lorraine shifted her feet beneath her chair like trying to regain her footing in reality. "Fire Roy?" Roy was a silver-level team member and second only to Lorraine in Employee of the Month Awards received. "Why did you do that?"

"This was corporate's call. You know I'd never fire Roy of my own accord. I've been told to thin the ranks, starting with highest paid team members."

Lorraine allowed herself a moment to resent the fact that Roy had been paid more than her, but he could cover Customer Service and her words piled up in the face of adversity. She refocused on Roberta. "Why did headquarters tell you to do that?"

"We're being shut down, Lorraine. The company is trying to keep from going under, so they're closing the biggest stores."

Lorraine watched Roberta's bright orange lips move, but the words didn't compute. None of them. She thought instead about how the neon hue made Roberta's mouth seem electric and wished that she were daring enough to wear the same color. *Mango, Darling.*

"Lorraine?" said Roberta. "Did you hear me?

"We're…closing?" Lorraine's mind raced to plug the hole in her understanding. "Is it because of the Hitler tea kettle?"

Back in 2013, the company had sold a teapot that people said looked like Hitler. Her father had fought against Hitler and

Lorraine didn't think the teapot looked like the Führer at all. At the time she'd surmised that Sears or Dillard's had pushed the narrative to try and steal market share and she still hadn't seen any evidence to exonerate them. Whatever the motivation, the damage had been done, and in the years since, Lorraine traced any problems within the company back to the kettle.

"It's not the tea kettle," said Roberta. "They're trying to avoid bankruptcy."

"By closing us? Don't you need money to avoid bankruptcy? How are they going to make money if they close us?"

"I don't know all the details, just what they've told me. Apparently, they think this is the company's best chance to survive."

"And it's…permanent?"

"For us it is."

Suddenly, Lorraine was back home inside the musty condo with her mom's threadbare flower-print furniture and Sudoku towers. She'd never find another Roberta; another someone who would see past her age and her eye and her speech. Without a job, she was just another old woman sitting in a chair in a room. Stumbling into the community pond with the crocodiles or whatchamacallits seemed a more desirable outcome.

Roberta reached across the table, snatching Lorraine's hands away from her mug. "Once I let Tabitha and Jamarcus go, it'll be just me, you, and three babies left to run the whole place, Lorraine." Babies was Roberta's term for anyone under thirty. "They're giving us two weeks. Clearance begins on Thursday."

The word was like hearing a terminal diagnosis. *Clearance.* And it was. For the store, for Lorraine. She stood, defiant. "Did they even come and see our store? How well it's run? The ratio we keep between stock and display? How we use our shelf space? Nobody comes close—not even marketing, I've seen the catalogue pictures, Roberta." She'd begun sweating again.

"Sweetheart. We're done. Two weeks. Then the doors close." Roberta had kind eyes and they were trying to make Lorraine feel better. "They say when one door closes, another opens."

The clearance sale came even though Lorraine had asked God to stop it.

That morning, she stared into the Buick's visor mirror, lipstick rising from her fist like a tiny popsicle on the verge of melting. The first day of the store's dying. A countdown to the end of the world. Maybe, if she stayed put, she could stop time. A bead of sweat fell from the tip of her nose, marking a perfectly round spot of burgundy on her scarlet blouse.

Snapping out of the daydream, Lorraine capped the lipstick and pushed out from the car. Walking past the guard house, she closed her good eye and let the bad one burn. Through the crooked shards of pained vision, a picture coalesced: a land cut right from a fairytale, an afternoon sky over a waterfall with the sun putting rainbows in the spray. She shut her eyes and let the sting dissipate. If only to go there. If only to go anywhere.

Customers milled about outside the store, even though it was an hour before opening. The front doors, once gleaming expanses of spotless plate glass, were now plastered with crooked yellow posters declaring the store's end like a retail obituary.

CLEARANCE SALE
GOING OUT OF BUSINESS!

UP TO 75% OFF
EVERYTHING MUST GO

The words cut, and Lorraine frowned and gritted her teeth as she entered. Someone tried to follow her inside. "Not open!" she snapped. "Yet...sorry."

Roberta raced back and forth beyond the second set of doors, putting signs into place atop racks of women's Fall coats. "Oh, Lorraine, good," she said, puffing her lips.

Lorraine had never seen Roberta so harried. It was almost more disconcerting than the ugly signs defacing the storefront. Any illusions Lorraine had of their branch being rescued were truly fantasy.

"They'll be here for everything, but clothes will go first. I need you in the change room. It'll be a zoo back there and I don't trust the babies to maintain order."

"What will the babies do?"

"I'll put Stacy on Home—if she shows up—Kevin on Menswear, Sanja on Women's. I'll float. It's gonna be a shitshow, Lorraine."

Lorraine grimaced at the use of curse words, but quickly forgave because Roberta was understaffed and deserved better.

Not five minutes after the doors opened, customers flooded the changing room, arms stacked with clothes swept in chunks from the racks.

Lorraine deftly guided them into stalls, abandoning any thought of enforcing the five-item maximum. Unpurchased items quickly clogged the rooms, which she cleared as best she could before others rushed in with what they'd hoarded.

Returning to the counter with a load she'd recovered from stall eight, she began folding and hanging. The quicker the turnaround, the more likely they'd sell and... She knew she was clinging to the foolish hope that if they did well enough, corporate would rethink their decision to close them. As skilled as she was in folding and hanging, there was no keeping up as the clothes quickly swallowed the counter and piled into a mound that would take her hours to get through.

Roberta swept in sometime later, already talking. "Lorraine? Just take your lunch in here, if you don't mind—" She paused, spotting Lorraine amid the mountains of clothes. "Oh my God."

Lorraine shrugged, hanging a blouse onto an extra rack she'd brought in. Roberta leaned over the counter to see the full extent of the disaster. She sighed and set her head down on her hands. "Why bother, Lorraine?"

A wave of heat splashed across Lorraine's face. Why bother? This was her life! Their life! The words tangled on her tongue before she could say it.

Roberta saw her anger. "Lorraine. My doll." She stepped aside as a woman from Room Six returned a collection of winter clothing. "You have to let it go. You'll die of exhaustion if you try to get all of this back out on display. Just clear the rooms out and..." she waved her hands helplessly.

"And give up?"

Roberta searched Lorraine's face. "Hey," she said, softening her voice. "If it helps you get through it, then...I don't see any harm. Get it *all* back on the floor if you want to, it makes no difference to me. Just please, take a break. And hey: if you see anything you like, set it aside. I'm making sure we all get our due for going through this."

"But—"

"The clearance pricing plus our employee discounts will bring this stuff to near zero anyway." She mimed some finger tapping. "The rest I can handle with my manager's override. Consider it your severance." She slid her arm behind the clothes that Lorraine had reassembled on the rack and lifted them from the rod. "I'll bring these back out on the floor."

Lorraine watched Roberta disappear into the hallway, then turned to the pile of coats returned by the woman. One of them was quite nice, a long, beige number with a narrow waist and a stylish hood. She eyed the rooms for any sign that she was needed and then took it up. *Where was it,* Lorraine wondered, *that she was planning to go with such a heavy jacket?* Somewhere faraway from Florida, that much was clear.

Defiantly, she thrust her arms into the sleeves, connected the zipper and yanked it to her neck, then flipped up the hood. She felt immediately idiotic, standing there in a coat she'd never buy, pretending to have a life she didn't have. Pathetic. She shut her good eye and let the bad eye burn.

An image appeared through the broken window of her vision. Triangles of blue and blinding white. But then the cracks melted away and the picture became clear. No longer was she a distant observer. It felt like she had leapt right into—

A blast of bitter wind stung her cheeks. Snow. A cloudless expanse of sky above. Turning in place, she was faced with a mountain. It loomed over her so high that it seemed ready to topple and flatten her into the earth. Terrified, panicking, she flipped the hood down. Then she was back in the changing room.

She scrambled to unzip the coat and let it drop to the ground. She rubbed her face against the lingering chill. A man emerged from Room One with some track pants and paused. He pulled a headphone from an ear and loud music pounded out. "Ma'am? You alright?"

The words piled up. Lorraine smiled bashfully and nodded. When he was gone, she doubled over and gasped for breath, then stood, wide eyed, heart pounding. The top of her head felt like it was being pulled into orbit. She couldn't place the emotions. It felt something like terror, but that was wrong. Her arms shook all the way to her shoulders. Her stomach fluttered. No, this wasn't terror. This was exhilaration. Euphoria.

An excited squeak leapt from mouth before she could stifle it.

She picked up the coat and flipped it around, inspecting it for…she didn't know what. She set it onto the counter and held her bad eye open again, until an image presented through the burning. It was like it had always been; swathes of color and shape obscured by fractured panes of stained glass. But when she donned the coat again, the mountain returned, bold and tangible as ever.

Quickly, she went to the pants that had just been returned, stepped them on, and hiked them up under her skirt.

A new place reflected clear in the lens of Lorraine's no-good eye. A musical darkness fringed in beams of colorful light. A cheering crowd. A rock band. Was she just watching or was she there? She poked a nearby reveler in the shoulder. They turned and yelled over the noise asking, annoyed, what she wanted.

"I just wanted to see if I'm here!" she answered.

"Yeah?" they said. "I'm not sure if you are."

Lorraine laughed. She wasn't hallucinating. She'd been transported. To a place from the customer's life? The present? The past? The music sounded like what had been pumping out of his headphones. Somehow, the clothes were a link to someplace real and the bad eye was parsing the destination.

Lorraine removed the pants and reentered the changing room. Before her, a teenager leapt backward with a gasp, and stumbled to the floor.

"Sweetheart!" said Lorraine, running over to check on the girl. "Are you okay?"

"The hell?" said the girl, jumping upright and scooting down the wall. "Are you messing with me or something?"

"Uh, no," said Lorraine. "What are you talking about?"

The teen pointed at her with a vaping pen. "You just...just...like. You like, just appeared in front of me."

Lorraine smiled warmly, then looked herself over. "I'm sure I didn't. I've been here all morning. It's the big clearance sale."

The girl glared at her vape pen, then rushed out of the room. Lorraine considered the heap of clothes left on the floor and marveled at what secrets they might hold. Not having the time to try on every garment that came back, she added the teen's jean jacket and leggings to the hoard behind the counter.

Just after five-thirty, Roberta trudged into the change room. "I don't know how we're going to do this for ten days straight."

Lorraine, noting that she didn't feel at all tired, continued briskly organizing returns. "It will be a challenge," she said, with every intention of meeting it. "You look exhausted." She ordered her words and added, "I'll do the register drops tonight so you can get home to rest."

Roberta looked at her like she'd just emerged from a cocoon. Lorraine felt like she had.

"I'm fine to stay," Lorraine continued enthusiastically, snapping a pair of slacks straight and securing the waistband to the trouser clamps. "I must have caught a second wind."

Roberta surveyed Lorraine's face, then raised her eyebrows, relenting. "Yes. Fine. I will take you up on that. Did you eat anything at all today?"

Lorraine *had* eaten—a delicious basket of fried plantains from a street vendor somewhere along the coast of Africa and a bowl of hot pot chicken on a hillside in China. "I had a little something, yes."

"Aren't you bright-eyed and bushy-tailed," said Roberta the following morning. "You didn't—you didn't stay here all night, did you?"

"Roberta," said Lorraine. "I wouldn't skip my nightly bath." She hadn't skipped her bath. She'd swum in the Mediterranean Sea just off the coast of Greece in a bathing suit tried on by a woman who had mentioned an upcoming trip to Crete.

The next nine days of clearance were much the same as the first, except that Lorraine now braved the waters of conversation with any person who would talk, eagerly peppering them with questions about their travels. This helped her decide which of their discarded try-ons to put in the Keep pile. If they'd been to a fascinating place, she held onto something they'd tried on. Amidst her elation, words came easier.

The locked-down doors and shuttered windows of Lorraine's world had blown open. Each day was a slide show, with tours of foreign lands done seconds at a time. She popped in and out of existence on the coastline of California, the prow of a fishing boat somewhere cold, a trail deep inside a tropical jungle, a fancy restaurant in a big city, a café in Vietnam.

The stock dwindled as the sale dragged on, and so did the crowds. Fewer folks were finding much to their liking, and eventually Lorraine was left on her own. Conveniently secluded in the change room, she made notes on the tags and organized the items according to geography, then made her purchases at the end of shift, and lugged them home. At night, she slept more soundly than ever, dreaming about the places she'd visited—ten lifetimes' worth in just a week—and upon waking, longed to return.

By the end, the store looked like it had caged a typhoon. No amount of running about by the few remaining employees had been enough to maintain order. Their time was at an end, with the corporate movers set to come in and clear out the rest.

Placing their keys in the cash register drawer, they headed toward the front, each of them carrying as much discount merchandise as they could. Kevin, whose arms overflowed with fancy sheets, karate-kicked a mannequin. Roberta laughed. Lorraine side stepped the rolling head without a thought, all pretense of decorum having melted away over the preceding days. That chapter of her life had ended. A new one was about to be written.

Lorraine hit the lights as the babies said casual goodbyes and rushed off to live their lives. She followed Roberta outside and waited as her ex-boss secured the deadbolts.

"They're making me mail the keys to corporate," she said, battling a lock. "Ridiculous."

Lorraine pointed to the pressure cooker sitting at Roberta's feet, the last of several small appliances the supervisor acquired during clearance. "I think you're even."

Roberta chuckled as she secured the final door and pocketed the key. "Yeah, you have a point. So...what are you going to do?"

Lorraine shook out her hands and picked up the swollen bags she'd carried out. "Oh, I'm going to do some traveling."

"Traveling!" Roberta laughed, shaking her head. "You don't even drive, doll. The only traveling you do is from this door to your mother's condo and back. What are you talking about, *traveling*?"

"One door closes and another opens. You said that."

"Honey, that's just what people tell other people when they get laid off."

"No," said Lorraine, "you were right."

"Whatever you say, doll." She gave Lorraine a hug. "Need a ride home with all that?"

"No thanks. I could use the fresh air," said Lorraine, backing down the walk. "I'll bring you back a souvenir!"

"I look forward to it."

The next morning, Lorraine sat in the Buick, a tightly packed duffle of clothes resting in her lap. The store was still laid out in her brain, but she'd pushed the products from the shelves and filled them instead with articles of clothing, each one signifying a new destination.

Her outfit was a purple warmup suit left in Room Two by a woman about her size, who had gone on and on about plans for a trip she took every year to a majestic spot in the mountains of Venezuela. Hearing the woman talk about it, Lorraine felt like she already knew the place, and took that as a nudge from the Universe.

She looked into the mirror and smiled despite the heat; despite the eye that didn't line up and the tongue that sabotaged her speech. She felt the weight of it all slip from her shoulders; her own limitations, her resentments. With her world grown large, all of that felt so small now.

From her pocket, she retrieved a brand-new tube of lipstick, color: *Mango, Darling.* She twisted it up, slathered her lips orange, then smacked them. She stowed the lipstick, took hold of the jacket's bright yellow zipper, and drew it to the top of the collar.

Her destination appeared in pieces through the prism of her eye, then suddenly she was there. A land cut right from a fairy tale. A waterfall with the sun making rainbows of the spray.

If you liked it, leave a comment. Authors love that!
Remember to subscribe to our e-mail updates so you'll know when new stories are posted.

About the story

The story is loosely based upon a relative of mine. I am very close to her and there is a good bit of her wrapped up in the character of Lorraine. For much of her life I feel she's been underestimated, underappreciated, and in a lot of ways nearly invisible. I wanted to tell the story of someone like that, because people like my relative don't seem on first glance to be main character material. They're overlooked by definition, usually in favor of a character who appears more dynamic on the surface.

A question for the author

Q: What's the story no one else thinks is as good as you do?

A: I'm going to suggest a story that no one thinks is as good as I do, but only because it's new and relatively few people have read it. It's a short novel called *Little Future, The Ghost* by Daniel Cohen and it's the most blistering satire of capitalism and technoculture I've ever read. Other than being satire, it's impossible to categorize, but utterly genius and thought provoking. Absolutely brutal.

About the author

Chris lives in Dallas, Texas with his wife and daughter. He does art, writes short fiction and novels, and occasionally practices law.

www.chrispanatier.com, @chrisjpanatier

The Frozen Generation

Jacob Coffin

Compared to my coworkers, I didn't get many death threats. Storage, my department, was usually overlooked by fanatics and politicians.

They saved their anger for the people up front who made the Frozen Generation — the doctors and administrators who met the clients, did the scans, fed in the waldos, extracted the mingled cells, vitrified them in cryofluid. My crew in Storage were just the ones who tended them forever after.

They had their reasons for overlooking us. The Frozen were an easy demographic to advocate for, and an easier population to have when it came time to allocate votes and funds. But most people in this state would still tell you that extraction destined for cryostasis was just abortion with less guilt. Those people had gotten their way tonight, expanded the definition of abortion to include any extraction not destined for immediate gestation. And banned it.

Their new laws were going to close the clinic, maybe for a long time. But that wasn't my main concern. They'd also upped the charges for embryonic deaths in an extraction clinic and, tonight of all nights, I'd received notice of a blackout across the entire facility.

That's why I was in my truck, racing back to work as fast as I could drive after only two hours of sleep and despite the crowds celebrating in the streets.

We had backups. We were a priority repair site by law. We were seriously overbuilt for the two-hour limit the power company had to have us fixed by. But my team would be scared, and I wasn't going to let them deal with this alone. After all, they knew as well as I did that technically, under the new laws, any failure onsite could cost us our lives.

I made some calls as I got on the freeway. The front office didn't answer. No one on my crew knew what had happened yet, except that the power was definitely out and only for us.

The protestors had probably just shot out a transformer. They did that sometimes when they were celebrating. Tonight, that was really the best-case scenario.

The scattered fireworks popping low over the rooftops, the crowds in the streets around the churches, and the 3 a.m. rush hour traffic were enough to tell me tonight wasn't a night for best-case anything. But I wasn't thinking clearly.

Cars were already filling up vacant lots in the industrial park we called home. Armed silhouettes with posterboard signs grouped together in the early-morning dark and chill. The usuals claiming their spots early, maybe. Either way they'd have a big crowd today — some of our neighbors even rented their lots to them.

I was scanning the parking lots as I went — more from habit than because of the news tonight. I like to think I've gotten pretty good at watching my surroundings, even when I'm tired and stressed. After a protestor follows you home, you find your motivation.

The crowd got thicker once I was close enough to see the place. The clinic had already been pretty ugly, sort of a warehouse trying to turn into a bunker, but it was folks like these who had put the finishing touches on it, decorated the outside with scorch marks and bullet-pocks.

Speaking of bullets: one of them took a shot at me.

I honestly hadn't been expecting that. The crowd at the gate didn't have the usual rage tonight, though they threw some rocks when I pulled through, just to keep up tradition. I figured they were there more to celebrate and maybe burn our building down later if the police seemed amicable. They'd won, after all; no more need for self-martyrdom.

But once I made the last turn toward the garage, my back windshield exploded.

I hit the gas and slammed down the ramp and out of view before I'd fully processed the gunshot. And then it was over and I was sitting there in the red emergency light of the employee garage with more adrenalin than I needed for work problems and nothing to use it on.

I ran my fingers over tufts of foam in the new hole in my roof while I called the shooter in to our security team. Though God knew what they could do about him. After that was done, it all started to feel real, and I had to pause and get my breathing under control. I knew from experience that if I stayed focused, I could save the real freakout for after I got home and felt safe. And I had a lot of work to do.

The bullet hole was barely in arm's reach. Not a very near miss. Had he been trying to kill me or just scare me and make me run? That pissed me off worse than attempted murder. I could picture them laughing and cheering while I fled out of sight.

If they'd known what department I worked for, would it have made any difference?

I got out, slammed the door, and climbed upstairs in the dark, checking my phone for updates to the alerts that had woken me.

Power failures were the last thing we needed now. Every other supplier we relied on had been flaking for weeks, including our cryofluid producer, now fifteen days late on our delivery. I think they saw which way things were going, knew nobody was going to enforce our protections any longer. Even when a company's official faith didn't oppose extraction, there were always employees who felt that helping us endangered their immortal souls.

No updates on the power alerts. My feed was full of articles on the new laws, but I ignored them.

Don't get me wrong, things were bad, but this back and forth had been happening for my entire life. Hell, this mess of shortcuts and simple solutions was the reason I even existed. As far as I was concerned, this was just a temporary interruption of service until the law got challenged or interrupted somehow.

Even the people who had passed it didn't seem to expect this to last forever. They'd already tried gestating every unwanted embryo and that led to the government hives they then spent decades tearing down, and generations of Unwanted like me who didn't even vote for them. Doing it again with even less planning would be a horrible mess, but banning extraction with no solutions at all would be even worse.

The new laws would make things difficult, but I was trying to focus on what I could control. And for us in Storage, it would be business as usual, more or less.

From here on out it was our job to keep the clinic operational until we could reopen. And new admissions would be on pause, which would give us some time to catch up on maintenance, build some new racks, maybe even upgrade our cryofluid production capabilities if I could mooch some budget while the rest of the work was on hold.

We'd get through this.

Inside, the place was in chaos. Half the lights were off and there were way too many staff here for this time of night. The lobby was locked down, galvanized drop-barricades reflecting the lights back through the glass doors up front.

Ester was cleaning out her desk, taking everything with her name on it. She'd actually grown up in the same hive I did, though she was a later generation, so she was a bit more normal. I was in a hurry, but she looked so freaked out I stopped when we made eye contact.

"Moses, did you hear Dr. Quarzi quit?" she asked. She had her fake-calm, air traffic control voice going.

"What?"

"Yeah, he called in and did it over the phone right after the hearing, from London. He said this will be a huge mess and we should all get out before it starts if we know what's good for us. He'd already cleaned out his files and everything."

I blinked, tired eyes bleary in the bright light, and looked down at her desk. "Taking his advice?"

"Yeah. How about you?"

"I just came in to fix the power. If this place doesn't stay cold, we're all in a lot of trouble."

She gave me this look. "We're in a lot of trouble either way. My boyfriend has family in Canada — we're heading up there. You should get out too."

Wow.

"Uh, best of luck," I said. "Look, you'll be okay, you just do inprocessing."

Still that flat look, like I didn't get it. I guess I didn't. "Yeah. Good luck yourself."

Man, I just kept everything cold.

I hustled through the office, looking for the Operations Director. If the power loss was upstream, then getting it back was her problem. The rest of us just had to keep the outage from harming the patients.

Most everyone I saw was hurrying and worried. Some were unpacking reserve Herz-Stanton exowombs, and the rest looked like they were leaving. I didn't recognize half of them. Sure, most of my work is back in Storage, but I come up once a day to check the tanks in the clinic, write up my maintenance reports, and order parts. I like to think I'm sociable, for a hive boy anyways.

I stopped outside the Ops Director's office. Charlotte was standing over her desk, shouting into the phone, gestures and everything.

She didn't show any sign of slowing down, and with everything else going on, I couldn't wait for answers. Whatever had caused this blackout, I had to check our status.

I headed for Storage, my department. There was a reason that the only clinics left in this state stored their patients on-site: Storage facilities got guarantees. With the nation's most vulnerable citizens in our vaults, reliant on their services, the power and telecom companies couldn't drag their feet for weeks when we got disconnected. More than that, we were allowed to hire armed security, and even got an exemption to the Religious Freedom Act so parts suppliers had to sell to us as long as we could pay. They accused us of a lot; I suppose hostage-taking was fair.

Storage took up most of our site. It was the big, bulky, warehouse-looking part of the facility with the legally-mandated symbols outside, to protect clinic bombers from killing any of the Frozen. Inside, there were thousands and thousands of silver cryo flasks linked with tubes and wires resting on rows of metal shelves, elevated flood-safe, suspended and stabilized against earthquakes and guarded by the most paranoid fire suppression system in the county. Each had an individual battery backup for its sensors and pumps and a small reserve tank of cryofluid.

The manifest for each flask listed the occupants by social security number. No names or assigned sex yet. For the vast majority it was far too early to identify more than the number of cells, and you could usually count those on both hands.

In the back, rising up over it all, was the in-house cryo distillation rig. The patients' storage tanks didn't take power to stay cold; they were just fancy vacuum flasks with sensors. But their cryogenic fluid evaporated in an endless slow boil, and we needed power to monitor the levels and to run the pumps that kept them topped off. The in-house 'still was elevated so we could rely on gravity feeds if we had to.

Cryofluid is pretty complicated stuff. It's mostly liquid nitrogen, but nitro on its own can be a vector for viruses and bacteria between tissue samples. Cryofluid has a mix of additives so we could transfer it safely and to assist with vitrification and devitrification. It was actually overkill for our purposes, as most of our patients were kept in hermetically sealed straws, but our state legislature said nothing was too good for the Frozen Generation (except hives of their own), especially if it made running this place difficult.

As I looked for my crew, I automatically checked the dashboard for each rack of tanks I passed, eyeing the levels and power requirements.

All the levels were lower than I expected.

Some of my techs were shouting over by the loading dock. Zeke saw me and waved me over, calling across the warehouse:

"Mose!" He looked worried, and that worried me.

"Zeke, what's going on?" I asked. "Someone cut the lines?"

"Yeah! The fuckin' power company!"

"What, on purpose?" That cold dread started working its way down my back. They wouldn't. They fucking couldn't.

"Yeah. Told Charlotte on the phone. Can't legally provide services."

"What, because of the abortion definition thing? We're not taking patients and even then it'd only apply to the front office, not Storage." Not us. But the whole place was linked together – that was how the clinic benefited from Storage, after all.

"Yeah. Closed the loophole."

"Loophole, hell. This was their goddamn solution in the first place."

Exowombs were supposed to solve abortion. Then when the flood of Unwanted got too deep, and government-commissioned hives had to raise the kids, cryostasis was their solution for that.

I ran my hands over my face. This was bad. Without power, our reserves and battery backups weren't overkill — they were woefully, criminally inadequate. We weren't an island. Weren't supposed to be. State laws enshrined us as a priority recovery site. Hell, they'd send the national guard if there were a flood or hurricane. Send 'em right past people trapped on their roofs or buried in rubble. Anything for the Frozen Generation.

But that had changed, hadn't it?

"Charlotte's been screaming at the power company," Zeke said. "The state police, the governor, even. Nothing's got us online. Been running on our solar reserves and gas gennys ever since. I had Jimmy making runs to the charge station for extra fuel, but once they figured it was for here, they refused to sell to him. I sent him to Pembrook since they're the next closest with liquid, but I'd be surprised if he doesn't just quit."

"If the main circuit's off, we're not generating new cryo. Hell, half the tanks are already low." We had solar rigs, but like everything else, they weren't enough to make us completely independent.

"I *know that*, Mose!"

These guys were looking to me because I had always been the quick one, the first with a solution when things went bad. Some people are wired for crisis situations, and I kind of loved them. And now I was flat-footed, slow. Tired. They needed me to be better. I shook my head to clear it.

"Okay, we need to cut everything we can, try to make the reserves last. Mike, hit the breakers, cut the whole front office. Keep the clinic for half an hour and warn the docs up front — I think they've got a couple active exowombs, and they'll need time to transfer back to cryo. We can move 'em back here on the battery backups if we have to.

"Zeke, Sol, get the pumps running. Top up all the flasks and shelf reserves first, and pump whatever we got left into the reserve tanks on the 'still."

"It won't last as long once it's distributed."

"Yeah but it won't do us any good in the main tanks. Sounds like we could end up running without *any* power for a while, so we need to get the patients as self-sufficient as we can. Same for power, make sure the tank batteries are all fresh.

Pull some from the vehicles if you have to."

It was the same protocol we were supposed to use if the ocean came in around us, or the building collapsed. Get all the cryotanks ready for travel and wait for the national guard to come collect us. We'd lose auto-refill when the generators stopped. Internal regulation and monitoring too, once the local batteries dried up. We could top off tanks manually, if we had any cryo left, and if we knew the tank was low. We'd have to make visual inspections.

If the outage lasted long enough, we'd have to start consolidating fluid.

After tonight, any embryonic deaths in an extraction clinic were to be charged as murder two. We could get first degree if it was the result of a deliberate action. That was starting to seem more possible than it had yesterday.

"I'll go talk to Charlotte and see about getting us some backup. Someone has to care." I tapped on a cryoflask. "They only just made a bunch of laws about these guys."

Everyone started moving, so that part of the job was done. We'd get this place set up as best we could and hope society at large would help.

I backtracked through the clinic, head down, through everyone's rush to prepare for whatever came next. Every now and then, security would call someone's name. Took me a bit to realize they were escorting people off-site.

I passed a couple of clinic techs opening up one of the equipment storage rooms. One had on the scrubs they all wear up front, the other just had jeans and a t-shirt. I thought I recognized them both from the day shift.

"What about the old Herz-Stanton Gen 20s?" the one in scrubs asked.

"Uh, they're not on the APL anymore," the other answered.

"But they still work fine, I mean, maybe keep them off the network but they'll do the job."

He wasn't wrong. I was born to a Gen 3 and even those were so safe that there were actual arguments over whether to ban internal birth because it killed too many Unborn Americans. It was a public health crisis, after all: when an

American's life begins at conception, failure-to-implant becomes the country's leading cause of death.

They don't exactly cover that stuff in school but I guess I have an interest, since their last great idea led to me being born Unwanted, named by an algorithm, and raised in a hive, even if it wasn't one of the bible-warrior training facilities/sweatshops you see in the documentaries.

"She said all the approved units. This is just CYA, right? They're looking for ways to screw us, so I don't think we'll get bonus points for going above and beyond using illegal equipment."

"Fair enough."

If they were starting up extra exowombs now, of all times, that would be a problem. But I'd deal with it once I knew when we'd get the power back.

I didn't hear any shouting as I approached Charlotte's office. That seemed like a good sign. This had to be some local fuckup. Some anti-extraction asshole at the power company giving us a hard time.

Charlotte was slumped forward on her desk, her tablet docked and playing some news feed. The smart wall to her left showed every angle of the perimeter and most rooms in the clinic. On the cameras, cars had filled the closest lots outside. Biggest crowd we'd seen in years.

I knocked on the door frame. "Hey boss, how's it going?"

"Hey, Moses. I thought I told you to go home and get some sleep." She gestured at the news. "'Cease all extraction operations. Commence the immediate and safe transfer of all Embryonic-Americans to external wombs and begin gestation.'"

I gave her the baffled, disappointed look we'd shared through so many newsreels of hearings and debates.

"Yeah, we'll get right on that."

There weren't enough approved exowombs on the planet for that. And even if they'd all been in the U.S., it'd take decades to get through the backlog.

We had twenty on site. We'd tried to order more over a year ago, after the election, but all the domestic manufacturing companies were swamped, and you couldn't buy them from overseas for fear of foreign supply-chain sabotage. Sleeper-diseases, hard-coded loyalties, who knew what the Reds could cook into our most vulnerable citizens?

And hospitals got legal priority on exowombs, of course. Most wanted births were external these days, if only for the legal liability. A miscarriage was bad enough without the criminal investigation ripping your life apart just in case.

"All the hospitals in a hundred-mile radius are already swamped." She said, "I've called every one of them. The other sites are dumping as many cases off on them as they can. I got St Mercy's to agree to a *hundred*, a lousy hundred kids! And then some assholes parked ten freezer trucks in their emergency lane and took off on foot. Now it's all, 'sorry, now *we* have six hundred thousand to take care of, good luck with yours.' It's like that everywhere."

"Any word on the power?"

She snorted. "All the words are bad. It's not coming back."

"Why?"

"Power and Light's lawyers dusted off a couple of old state abortion laws from back around the fight over the amendment. Any organization or individual who provides aid or assistance *of any kind* to an abortion clinic will be held equally liable. Apparently, it doesn't matter that we're not taking clients anymore. Our lawyers think their interpretation is legit enough to stick until we've challenged it in court."

And if things kept going like this we'd all be in jail for mass manslaughter or negligent genocide or something by then.

"The storage facility protections-" I started.

"One law says they have to provide power, the other says they can't." She paused just long enough to solidify her composure. When you do her job, you can't ever risk it slipping — there're always cameras on you looking for ammunition. "Our lawyers are still with us, and they're raising hell best they can." She said, "The ACLU and opposition legislators too. But by the time this mess gets sorted out, it'll be too late."

"They- they realize that if we shut down all the way, the embryos will thaw, right?" I asked. "And thawing would be bad for them?"

She shrugged again, like she didn't want to give the lawmakers or God's power company that much credit. These were the kind of people whose idea of compromise had forced generations of women who'd otherwise have taken a pill to risk surgery.

"Why are they doing this? They have to know it'll blow back on them…"

She looked down at the tablet, head in her hands, and said the next part almost to herself. Like she was thinking aloud. "There's a census coming up."

"Boss?" I didn't like this line of thought.

"If six hundred thousand 'people' disappeared overnight, they could redraw the map. Eliminate this district, a progressive congressional seat, and who knows how many state-level positions. It'd change funding allocations and…" She looked up at me. "Or maybe they're just a bunch of zealots who didn't listen when we pointed out all the problems with the bill six months ago, including that this could technically happen, even if it seemed unlikely. Same results either way."

She scrolled back through the news footage, picked out a segment, and spun the tablet. The Reverend Senator Callahan was walking out of the capitol building, a wide, closed-mouthed smile serene on his face.

"It's about personal responsibility. To all those… facilities, I'd say you shouldn't have done the procedures if you couldn't take care of your obligations afterwards. The American people trusted you with their children, and if anything happens to any single one of them, we *will* hold you accountable. At long last."

"Oh."

That was all I could think to say. I'd missed something Ester and Dr. Quarzi had seen coming.

I knew they'd been trying to kill our industry. What I hadn't realized was that it wasn't about the Frozen Generation. They were after us.

Us, like as individuals, the people who worked at the clinics. Not just the politicians who supported us, or our CEO, or the other executives they dragged before congress, but all of *us*. Me.

Even after all these years in their crosshairs I'd still taken them at their word. Still internalized some gut, cultural-suffusion belief that they cared about the Frozen Generation enough not to sabotage them. No matter how much they hated extraction or us that enabled it, Storage should have been safe.

Oh. You damned idiot.

It wouldn't matter if tonight's ban got overturned if we were all in prison when it came time to reopen the clinic. Whether we were the victims of a conspiracy or yet another bit of collateral damage didn't really matter. Dr Quarzi was right. Ester was right. For all the good it would probably do them, at least they were running.

"How long do we have?" Charlotte asked.

I shook out of the reprieve; the math was fresh in my mind. We were already so low.

"Without more juice? Maybe a day or two before we start losing ones near the top of the flasks to evaporation."

With cryo, thawing isn't like you'd imagine. Everything's so cold, it's actually skipped freezing to being this ice-free glass. If it thaws unregulated, you have two problems: ice crystals will form and slice all the cells apart, and the cryoprotectants that preserve the cells by replacing their water will go toxic as they warm. Warming the cells and diluting out the cryoprotectants is a whole process you just can't manage when a few thousand flasks of enhanced nitrogen are going from liquid to gas and you have no electricity.

"I contacted our sister organizations and sent out an alert on all our social media. Described what they're doing and begged for fuel and cryo," Charlotte said. "We've got a good base of someday-parents who are organizing to help."

"Any luck?"

"Not sure if our people can even get through that riot outside. The police are supposedly here to keep things under control, but they're basically blockading us in."

My eyes were still on the muted tablet, watching our representatives. I felt a bleak certainty that there would be plenty of investigations to determine all the ways we were at fault for this.

The power cut out. The wall of security monitors went dead. The only light in the room was the screen on the tablet.

I shook out of it. "Oh, yeah. I had Mike cut everything but Storage. We'll move any clinic hardware we have to keep to the back, try to make it last."

Charlotte nodded. "Good idea."

"Could you double check the doors?" I asked. "Some of the emergencies are fail-open maglocks and we might need to barricade them."

"Sure." She grabbed a flashlight from her desk and the gun she kept holstered under the tabletop. She knew about the doors. She was probably relieved to have the distraction.

"Thanks."

Mike caught me as I left Charlotte's office.

"It's Dr. Clarke. She won't let me cut the clinic. Says she wants any surplus for the wombs."

"What? Tell me she hasn't started a new batch."

Those things suck power and they still take almost nine months per kid. Regulations imposed on the manufacturer — anything else would be unnatural. And there were only twenty of them. We had over six hundred thousand embryos and fetuses in the back.

"Sorry, boss. She outranks me."

"What, she's gonna print half a million kids before the batteries run out?"

But she had to look like she'd tried. She was the doctor in charge of production. Someday they'd be asking her, 'Why didn't you try to save *any* of them?'

We were on a sinking ship, and we were all looking ahead, past the lifeboats to the historians, trying to dictate what they'd say about us in their accounts.

Or, more likely, in our atrocity trials.

All twenty Securus Platinum exowombs were humming away on their pedestal mounts, and ten old Herz-Stanton 25s were sitting on the counter. All were occupied and lit.

I wondered where Dr. Clarke had gotten the kids. Were they future orders? Had she picked them at random? The front office tried anonymizing the embryos once. Give them all an equal chance at adoption. Our client rate had plummeted. People out in the world talked a big game about the abandoned, forever-frozen masses and their right to life, but when it came time to grow their new kid, they only wanted the best.

"Dr. Clarke?"

"I knew you'd show up." She looked tired and scared. She pointed her phone at me like it was a gun. Recording the conversation, proof she'd done all she could. Proof I was the bad guy here. Fine. Her jury would love us turning on each other.

"Doctor. You need to put the patients back into cryostasis." It's always 'the patients' when you talk about the Frozen, but especially when you know you're on video.

Her chin came up and her face went hard. "This is my department, and these patients' well-being is my responsibility. I have to do what's best for them. I don't answer to the cryotechs."

Ouch.

"They cut our power, and these things are draining the reserve." I spoke clear and slow for the court. "Without the exowombs running, we can get another day or so for all the patients in the back. Maybe they'll turn the power back on by then. If we don't, they'll *all* start to thaw." She didn't react, so I kept going. "We'll never have enough power for these machines either way. But running them could kill all the patients onsite."

I half expected her to say I was just trying to save my own department at her expense, but she didn't go there. She stuck to the script.

"The law says we need to transfer all Unborn Americans to exowombs immediately."

She put herself between me and them, like she expected us to fight.

I realized I didn't have to argue this out. I didn't have to say anything. The breaker was in the basement.

Antisocial hive tendencies, I guess. We always caught flack for being 'indirectly confrontational' after being raised by a monolith we couldn't affect in the slightest. As a nod to professionalism, I spoke up on my way out.

"Okay. You can put them back in cryo or you can take them someplace else. Either way, I'm cutting power to this room." I headed for the stairwell. She followed me.

"They can't leave these facilities! They're not allowed to leave the clinic. We have to maintain custody of all-"

I stopped at the basement door while I found my light. "I can spare a truck. I can't spare power."

"You don't 'spare' anything! That's not your decision to make!" I was the last facilities person here with any rank, so I would contest that.

Luckily, I didn't have to. Charlotte appeared from the darkness and stepped in. I guess we hadn't exactly been arguing quietly.

"Rachel. Stop," she said. There was an edge to her voice, but she kept it calm, authoritative. "We can't support them here. Not anymore. If you want them to make it, you have to take them someplace else."

"But they can't leave…"

She took Dr. Clarke's hand. "Listen, they, and you, will be safer someplace else. Take them to a hospital, take them to your church. Hell, take them to the governor's mansion. Anywhere'll be better." She started guiding her toward the garage. "Come on, I'll help you get a truck."

"I-"

"It's *okay*. It's okay. These are terrible times and you've done everything you could. If we had more than thirty exowombs, you would have saved even more. You've already gone above and beyond. They'll understand. Hell, you'll probably be a hero."

I hit the staircase, flashlight searching for the clinic breaker. I'd probably be able to watch her single-handedly rescue those thirty innocent lives again someday in the based-on-a-true-story dramatization. From my prison cell.

I made a decision on my way back to Storage. Or maybe I realized that I'd made it a while ago.

Keeping the Frozen 'alive' had always been the goal, but the way I'd seen it, my real job was to keep everything perfect back here, exceeding every regulation, so nobody went to jail.

Most of the crew I had left seemed to feel the same way. If we quit, we'd be abandoning our teammates, and the rest of the clinic.

That made what came next easier. My plans might have changed since the drive in, but I'd still be doing my job.

Zeke was manually forcing the heavy door to the employee garage when I got back to Storage.

"Jimmy's back, and he says he got fuel!" Sol told me.

Zeke grinned. "I love that kid."

The sun was up now. I saw a sliver of it as the garage door rumbled back down. The truck rolled to a stop as we all hustled over.

Jimmy shoved the door open and stumbled out, looking beat and wild-eyed. "I'm sorry, boss." He shook his head. "I couldn't get- it's bad out there."

His knuckles were scraped bloody and he had a nice shiner forming on his left eye. He'd stopped somewhere and spray painted over the logo on the truck. I wondered if it was before or after his fight.

I went around the back and looked over the bed of gas cans. Most of them were empty.

Zeke was talking to him. "Hey, hey it's okay. You're okay."

"No, it's not. They'd only sell me eighty gallons. I couldn't do more, I'm sorry. The first place, when I tried to fill everything, they figured it out and came out with a gun. I-"

Behind us, Sol swore and kicked the truck.

"Hey, it's fine!" I waved a hand at him, then looked back to our driver. "You did more than we had any right to ask. It's okay. We'll figure something out."

There was a half second of silence, and then: "I quit." Jimmy was looking down at the painted-over logo, focus distant. "Look," he said. "I just came to get my truck. Sorry." He met my eyes for a second. "Sorry. I'm done. I got to go."

And then he did.

We got as ready as we could with what we had left. We consolidated the fuel, shifted our resources around so we weren't producing any more power than we could use or store, made sure we were running everything else on the minimums.

They worked hard, though they looked scared, kept checking their phones. Couldn't hold that against them today. News updates, worried texts from families. Finally, I said, "Enough. Go home. We're as ready for shutdown as we're going to get."

After all the hassle from the government inspections, the impossible hours from being badly understaffed, the slurs and attacks and violence from the protestors, the crew I had left were here because they were loyal and they cared. With their skills, they could have gotten jobs at any lab or factory floor for more pay and less work, less stress. I was grateful for them.

"Naw, you'll need us here," Sol said.

"I need you to go get some sleep. Go home, see your families. I'll text you if we need anything else. There'll be a lot to do when Charlotte and her lawyers get the power back. They'll probably have inspectors out here before the next shipment of cryo."

"What about you?"

I didn't have kids, or anyone at home to worry about. Most of my forty-six surviving hive siblings could take care of themselves.

"I'll take the first shift here. I'll let you know as soon as anything changes, or if I need help with anything in the meanwhile."

"If the power doesn't come back…" Zeke started.

"I'll watch the levels. I got reserve batteries, reserve tanks, and gravity feeds from the 'still. If I need a bucket brigade, I'll let you know."

They laughed a little. Then they just looked tired. Finally, they took the out, headed for their trucks. Promised they'd look for gas, be back as soon as we needed them. But they weren't coming back and we all knew it. I wasn't going to text them, and they knew that, too.

Someone had to be responsible for what was going to happen next. Storage was my department. If I sent them away before the failures began, it kept responsibility for everything nice and tidy.

I waited till they were gone, then I climbed up on the pump station, set all the warning alarms to max volume, and took a nap.

I woke up when I started sweating through my clothes. The sun was cooking on the warehouse roof — good for our solar, not that it'd do more than pump our thin reserves around. The Frozen wouldn't notice this heat though, not in their vacuum flasks of liquid nitrogen. Out here it was too hot, but in there it was impossibly cold.

The generator's warning lights glowed amber on the dash. Nothing left to do about that.

I went for a walk around the clinic.

The place was empty, trashed in everyone's haste to evacuate. I could hear someone clinking around in one of the labs and it made me think of rats or squatters. Just last night it had been business as usual, and now this. Muffled outside, I thought I could hear voices and pops, like fireworks or gunshots.

Amerinews was playing in Charlotte's office.

"State militia units here in Godless California are mustering on the border for what they call a humanitarian mission, an invasion to kidnap and illegally transport the Frozen across state lines. It's a logistical nightmare in clear violation of state autonomy. God only knows what will happen to these helpless babies."

"Hey, Moses," Charlotte said.

"Hey. Jimmy quit."

"Everybody's quit."

We both looked at the tablet for a minute.

"How about you?" I asked.

"I'm going down with the ship. You?"

"I'll keep things cold as long as I can. After that, I don't know. Any luck on the power?"

She shook her head. Subject change. "There's a mob outside."

"Yeah? Maybe we'll get lucky and they'll set the place on fire. Take the credit." I said.

That got a little smile. "If you need to get out, the side door by client parking still opens out. Plus your loading dock."

"Thanks. Not sure there's any running away from this."

"Nope."

She sat there in the dark, lit by her dwindling tablet. "I'll be here if you need anything," she said.

I walked back to Storage and made my rounds again. Looked over all the racks and racks of flasks, batteries, reserve tanks, bundled wires and tubing. I'd configured most of these units. I'd loaded half of them. Tended them all for years, watched for even a single power or temperature failure. Soon there'd be thousands.

The last generator sputtered to a rest outside. The fans stopped. The pumps cut out. The beeps and squawks of the monitors went dead on standby. And in the silence, the Frozen Generation began to thaw.

If you liked it, leave a comment. Authors love that!
Remember to subscribe to our e-mail updates so you'll know when new stories are posted.

About the story

"The Frozen Generation" started with an internet argument somewhere in early 2019. Buried in among the various hot takes on some now-forgotten reddit thread was the confident opinion that abortion as an issue would soon be over. Artificial wombs, it said, would allow for the adoption of unwanted embryos without impacting anyone's bodily autonomy.

There are plenty of straightforward issues with this modest proposal, starting with the fact that bodily autonomy and forced surgery aren't exactly compatible, but I tend to be a bit engineer-minded, so I was caught as much by the sheer number of logistical issues.

I never responded to that particular discussion, but there was something about the concept I couldn't leave alone. Simple solutions to complex problems, especially when their proponents won't consider the ways it could go wrong, or the cost to everyone around them, tend to really bother me. I feel like I keep seeing this belief that because something is the Right Thing To Do that it couldn't possibly hurt anyone, or that the people it'll hurt don't matter.

So I started iterating through the obvious issues and thinking about the solutions society would have to implement to fix them, and then the problems those solutions would cause next. By May 2019, this world-building exercise had formed the backbone of "The Frozen Generation".

I almost always start with the concept then kludge the plot on afterward. In this case, Mose, his coworkers, and their bad night fit nicely into the latest in the rolling series of man-made disasters I'd charted out, and gradually stole the show, as the plot ought to do. My beta readers, sensitivity readers, and *Metaphorosis's* editor were a huge help in bringing out everyone's personality and making clear their motivations, both good and bad.

My worldbuilding goal throughout the piece was to take the concept of a setting with ectogenesis 'solving' abortion and to stretch it to its breaking point, to find as many weird circumstances, edge cases, and exploits in the concept as possible. As for my main goal, I wanted to show the human cost of these nights, and to do all that extrapolation while handling the subject respectfully and thoroughly. I hope I managed it. There were a few things cut or reduced that I may end up exploring elsewhere, like the right to not reproduce (currently often bundled in with bodily autonomy, but an issue which would quickly become distinct in this setting) or even just the human cost of this 'solution', the risk and pain of forced surgery, or it's alternative, forced birth, which was mostly left in this version's background.

About four thousand words worth of backstory and essay-like rants have been cut, much to the story's benefit. The setting's backstory, from the introduction of artificial wombs, to the hives, to their replacement with cryostasis, and all the factions of conservative opponents to the 'abortion' of the day were spelled out in tedious detail, until one of the last drafts. Cut with that was the overtly-stated theme that laws only exist if someone will enforce them, that norms, conventions, and traditions are utterly worthless. This message became less important to explain once the Supreme Court demonstrated it more effectively than I could ever hope to.

I learned a lot as I researched this story. About cryostasis, in vitro fertilization, and religious beliefs around same, but I think I was most struck by the artificiality of the abortion debate itself, something I hadn't even known about when I started out. It seemed my history classes had skipped the efforts of Paul Weyrich, Jerry Falwell, and C. Everett Koop and others in the 1970s to teach then-fairly-apathetic evangelicals (even using a film tour) to see abortion as an affront to God, just as a step towards building the Moral Majority. There is no technological solution to an issue like that.

I went into this story well aware that I was manifestly unqualified to write it. I often am — I frequently write characters with experiences I've never had, police detectives, post-apocalyptic survivors, MMA fighters, my stories are full of roles I've never held. But this time it was important. I don't have a uterus. I don't work in a health-care field. I'm not directly impacted by this fight. I've done my best to keep this story to an outside perspective, to research everything carefully, and to avoid talking over anyone or trying to write anyone's experience for them. Hopefully I managed that too.

A question for the author

Q: Duckbilled platypus – result of divine distraction, or alternate universe crossover?

A: I can only hope for an alternative reality where the platypus is perfectly mundane; an entire ecosystem of egg-laying, bird-part-having, venomous mammals, where all the no doubt equally strange and venomous human-analogues are baffled by the humble Australian woodchuck or whatever we were supposed to get. I'd like to trade books and movies with that alternate dimension.

About the author

Jacob Coffin is a sci-fi writer with a passion for land conservation, reuse, and human rights not being rolled back.

jacobcoffinwrites.wordpress.com,
@jacobcoffin@writing.exchange

The Numismatist

Cecelia Isaac

On a lonely day on the river, a soul awaited me by the bank. The mists were high, and I saw no others as I angled my craft through the water to the shore.

The seeker entered the river. The hood of their cloak obscured their face. Water crested over their boots and wet their hem.

I reached out a hand. The seeker caught it, and I used my pole as a counterbalance as I hefted them into my boat. Mortals view me as a wizened old man. This is a form only, and my strength is more than enough to bring my passengers in.

"Obliged," said the seeker in a muted voice. They produced their obol and passed it to me.

I took it up and placed it into an inner fold of my robes. Then I gripped my pole and leaned into it, using my weight to push us off.

My craft pulled achingly away from the banks as if meaning to keep us there. As the current was just about to catch us, I caught notice of a dusty residue on my fingers.

In the millennia I have performed my role, I have seen every currency imaginable. Faded and cheap or crisp and weighty; coin no longer used by the time the seeker passed or coin as commonplace as river stones. Some placed jewels on their tongues, thinking the larger the offering, the kinder the shore. But in their faces I saw all their lives, and knew exactly where they were meant to spend their eternities.

But today, lulled by the current or perhaps the untold years of routine, I had not even looked at the seeker's obol before accepting it.

My fingers darted back into my robes and fished out the obol. It was a small chunk of barley bread, hardened after days uneaten. I looked up as the seeker did, and our eyes met. As my face tightened, theirs folded into a look of almost-hauteur.

"Well, I tried," the seeker said.

I drove my pole into the mud, arresting our motion. The seeker threw out their hands against the rocking of the boat.

I admit I was used to more begging. When they said no more, I lunged forward and latched onto the seeker's arm. I tossed them bodily into the water and felt a glimmer of satisfaction when the seeker cursed and sputtered.

"Was that necessary? My cloak—!"

I anchored my boat and leapt to the bank as the seeker sloshed through the muck onto dry ground.

"Oh," they said. "I thought you couldn't leave the boat..."

I straightened, and their eyes went wide. Over a head taller than any seeker on the misty bank, even in the body of an old man I struck fear into the hearts of wise souls.

Unfortunately, I was not standing in front of one.

"Look..." The seeker spread their hands, and finally I identified their disposition. They were unrepentant. Not defensive, not mournful, not desperate. Desperation I saw every day. Those without loved ones, with no one to place the obol in their mouth, knew their fates were sealed. And yet they begged. This seeker had no intention of doing so.

I interrupted them. "This—" I held up the hunk of bone-dry bread, "—is not sufficient fare."

"And I know that. But you see, I didn't have anything else and—"

I walked away. Seekers without the fare spend 100 years on the banks. We had nothing more to say to each other.

Or so I thought. But the next day, the seeker waited to board with three other souls.

On the banks, there is but scarce difference between night and day. All is shrouded in mist, and trapped souls must exist in this twilight on the slim strip of land between the river and the cavern wall. Newly arrived seekers huddled together near the single wooden post that marked the pickup point, their shoulders hunched against the mist, protecting their obols.

Despite the dim light, I knew the seeker immediately.

"No," I said before they could open their mouth.

"I haven't said anything!" The seeker protested.

I gave them a skeptical look.

This was no hindrance to the seeker. "I know what the rules are, sir, but have you ever thought—"

I boarded my craft and pushed off from the bank as the seeker continued to speak. "—of bending them? There must be some sort of solution—"

The next day, they took a new tack. "You'll find it was a mistake, sir. You see, my mother *meant* to place the coin, but a graverobber came shortly thereafter. I saw it all from a ghostly space, too incorporeal to do anything to assist my mother as she fought the dastardly—"

Their voice faded as the boat met the current.

And the next day: "Perhaps I could work for my keep, sir. Pray you rest your weary limbs while I take up the pole myself—"

And the next: "Fancy a wager? We could bet on it. I myself was well known as a card dealer, and would be happy to

show you the basic rules of Pitch and Toss
—"

And the next: "Is bread not a noble offering, sir? Do our bakers not toil to produce the best? I offer you a piece made of the finest my humble city has to offer —"

Usually, I kept order on the banks with the subtlety of a hammer. Most souls only needed one reminder to adhere to the rules. But this seeker danced out of range on light steps before darting back in for another attempt. Odd as our exchanges were, it was rare for me to have any form of exchange at all, and certainly nothing so upbeat.

I turned away again, but against my will, the corner of my mouth tipped up in a smile.

In the evening, I stowed my boat and returned to my abode. My home was built into the stone of the cavern wall. A little window faced the banks of the river, but overall my abode had a cave-like quality to it. This mattered little to me. I was used to the semi-darkness of the banks.

I had been to the Upper World before and found no enticement there. This home had all I needed: a warm fire to keep out the damp, a pallet to rest on, a store of nourishing food. I did not know why the seekers thought so often of the Upper World. Needs were softer here, less tangible. With time, one did not feel the pangs of hunger as strongly, nor the pain of injury.

And I had my collection. My abode extended back from the main rooms, where a heavy iron door opened into a storage tunnel lined with cases. Within each of these cases lay hundreds of obols in padded rows. All had been cleaned, catalogued, and stored by me. Thousands of years of tolls paid to me for my labor.

I brought out the day's offerings and began my work. I washed and dried them, sometimes using a pick to clean dirt from the ridges. I weighed and sized the coins, noting their details in thin lines in one of my notebooks. The oil lamp kept a steady light while I used a magnifying glass to examine the coins for fine details and faded faces of rulers and gods. Each was a record of the world beyond, and I glimpsed slivers of it through these tokens. More than a payment, they were a record of a world both intimately close and yet eons distant from me. It pleased me to tidy the mess of humanity into order.

When I was done, I opened a case and placed the coins gently inside, next to those from the day before.

Sometimes, if I had the time, I would unlock the storage tunnel and take down a case from generations previous. I found the corresponding notebook pages as well. I checked for damage or wear, of course, but I also just liked to look. In this way I saw a continuum. Obols gleamed in the light, their form changing from year to year, decade to decade. I wondered what would come next.

The next day, a fight broke out as I helped a line of souls into my craft. Two seekers began to shout. An obol fell to the ground and they lunged for it. I propped my pole against my craft and strode to them. Tearing them apart, I looked in their faces. But neither was the irrepressible seeker. I dropped the two and whirled about.

Sure enough, my boat had been discharged from the shore and was drifting away, helped by none other than the seeker who'd plagued me these last days.

I narrowed my eyes. In the next instant, I stood on the boat. The souls aboard gasped and recoiled, and even the seeker drew back in sudden alarm.

"How did you—"

Their next words were lost as I flung them, again, from my vessel.

By the time they dragged their cold, wet body to the shore, I was already there. Vibrating with anger, I grabbed the front of their cloak and lifted. Their feet left the ground. Their hood dropped back. They scrabbled at the clasp as the neck tightened around them.

The pale light fell on their face. Their left eye was newly blackened, and a cut covered in dried blood ran above that same eye. Had it happened when I threw them? No, the bruise would not have formed so quickly. And now that I looked more closely, I realized this cloak was not the same one as the day before. It was thinner and more worn, and had easily soaked through.

I set the seeker down. "What happened to you?"

The seeker's face changed, becoming closed and mulish for the first time. "My bad luck follows me even after death, it seems."

The banks were no easy place to spend one hundred years. Between the mists, desperate gangs roamed. They took what they wanted, seeking the cold comforts of material possessions. Though they did not eat, seekers still felt the echoes of other mortal needs. They fought amongst each other for weapons or clothing, or even territory. Detritus from the river, items they'd managed to carry from the Upper World—nothing was too small to feud over. I ignored these squabbles. Eventually, each soul's edges smoothed like a rock under the pressure of time.

The seeker was new to the banks, and yet I had seen their whole life's story when I first looked into their face. They were no stranger to sleeping with one eye open.

"You must better protect yourself here," I said. The words felt inane even as I spoke them. Why was I assisting a seeker? I was merely their ferryman, whose only role was to take their payment , not become involved in the petty disputes of those who could not afford my services. Familiar as this seeker's face had become, their existence was not my responsibility.

The seeker gave me a look that confirmed I'd been little help. "Just need a friend or two to watch my back, is all. Everyone here's a little flighty. Don't worry about me. I don't seem to feel hungry much anymore, so there's no need for all my teeth now anyway."

"You will heal," I said. "Faster than you would have in the Upper World."

They harrumphed.

We stood in silence.

"You will adjust, seeker."

When the seeker spoke, they did so grudgingly. "My name is Achem."

"You have no name here, seeker," I said as I turned. "Everything you were is gone."

They spoke to my back: "And yet the pain feels all the same."

In the morning, the seeker leaned against the prow of my upturned vessel where it was stowed on the shore.

"So, this is where you go at night."

Their voice had returned to its usual bright tenor. Their bruise had lightened already. Seekers did not often find my abode. It was far from the populated areas of the banks. That, and most souls preferred to give me a wide berth. But given this particular seeker's resourcefulness, I was not surprised to see them here.

"What is today's ploy?" I asked guardedly.

The seeker chuckled. "I thought I might rest a day. I can afford to take a day off if I'm going to be here one hundred years."

The morning was light, and the mist had cleared somewhat. The day felt almost fresh, despite the mugginess brought by the river and the looming cavern walls, and the fact that the sun never shone here.

"What happens if your boat is damaged?"

"Or stolen?" I asked with some indulgence. Maddening as Achem was, their resourcefulness had begun to charm. The seeker flashed an unrepentant smile. "I have the means to fix it, in my abode."

"You manage all yourself?"

Taking the sides of my boat, I turned the whole thing over so it sat right side up. Before I could make to push it into the water, the seeker began brushing off sand and mud from the edges. Though my vessel was a sacred thing, I confess to never having cleaned it. It was much the worse for wear.

The seeker completed their task as best they could, and then helped me push my craft into the water.

They clapped their hands in satisfaction. "When you return, I can spend more time on it. I bet we could make it look much better."

I frowned at their attentions. I did not think I had done anything to deserve them. But I did not refuse the help. I left them and poled down the river, to the path from the Upper World and my new arrivals.

Almost every day, some souls came whose one hundred years had concluded. They were free to mount the ferry to their final destination.

On this day, two were there. I recognized them without effort. They had not aged, of course. But they were hollowed. Their personalities had become worn and thin. These shades no longer fought amongst themselves. They felt nothing, not the cold, not the pain. Their mouths and hands twitched and grasped, seeking unknown succor.

I let them mount first, so they would know their place was guaranteed.

When I looked into their faces, I saw nothing left.

After the day had ended, I returned upstream to my abode. On the banks, souls who had arrived late begged to be ferried away, but I ignored them.

I dragged my craft to the shore. The seeker, Achem, appeared almost at my elbow. They bounced on their heels with an exuberance I had come to expect from them, no matter the task.

"Do you have cleaning supplies?" Achem asked.

I collected some tools from my abode while Achem inspected the boat. They gave me an arch look when I produced a bucket containing a random collection of rusted and disused boating implements.

I was surprised to feel a sheepish flash of emotion. "I may have more inside."

Achem followed me back to my abode this time. They lingered at the threshold while I went to my desk, where I kept the tools I used to clean my obols.

"What is that for?" Achem asked curiously.

I explained as I rifled through my things. "My work station. Where I care for and sort my collection."

Realization dawned on Achem's face. "Your collection. Every obol is here?"

"Of course." I gestured at the iron door that led to the storage tunnel. "Where else would they be?"

"So this whole time… you've just had a collection of riches in there? You must have *millions* of obols."

I moved the case I'd been working on the night before and grabbed the stack of rags behind it. "I suppose."

"Are they protected? By magic or other powers?" Achem asked.

"Yes," I responded. "Me."

Chuckling, Achem accepted the new tools as I ushered them out and closed the door behind us.

They checked each item fastidiously, then selected two scrapers. "I'll take the left, you can start on the right."

Bemused, I obeyed the instructions.

"You have no experience with boats," I said as we toiled. It was not a question; I knew the broad details of their life in the

Upper World. And yet, they worked with confident strokes across my craft.

Achem shrugged. "It's the same as cleaning anything else. And meditative, don't you think?"

I agreed. I had begun to realize the task was similar to the care of my obols, and was surprised to learn Achem felt the same sense of peaceful purpose.

"Do you know everything about me?" Achem asked after a time. "The others say you can see our lives."

"I know it from the moment I see your faces."

"And you remember everything? Everyone?"

I nodded. This was a lie on my part. I remembered everyone, that was true. But while I could see their lives, the details were not clear, not in the way the seekers assumed. I grasped impressions and fleeting scenes, much in the same way their memories were constructed.

And while I knew where on the far shore to deposit the souls, it was not I who made the judgment. Their actions while alive sealed their fates. I simply delivered them to their destinations.

After some time, Achem cleared their throat. "You didn't see Joa pass through, did you?"

The moment the name was said, a seeker's face rose to my mind. Their history played before me, but this time a familiar face appeared in some scenes—Achem, full of life.

"Yes."

"He's... he's not on the banks, is he?"

I shook my head. "They paid their fare and I ferried them across."

Achem sighed, their shoulders dropping. "Well... good."

"You are not pleased."

"I... am. I mean, he vanished, you know? I never saw him again. But I had hoped... I had some sort of dream. That he'd gotten out. And was living an idyllic life. Maybe as a farmer." Achem laughed harshly. "That was stupid, I see now."

They grieved, but I did not see why. "All of that is gone now. None of it matters anymore."

Achem was silent for a moment. "That isn't quite true yet."

We worked together in contemplative silence, first scraping, then waxing using wax found in a forgotten corner of my storage room, then cleaning out the interior with broom and cloth. Achem did not tire until the job was done. Finally, they sat back and spread their hands. I could only assume they were pleased with the job, even though no amount of care could disguise the vessel's advanced age.

I had been lulled into a calm as the evening pressed on and the shadows deepened, but now I wondered if Achem would expect something for this work.

My worry was short-lived. Achem returned the tools to the bucket and declared the boat had probably never looked better. "Until tomorrow," they said with a wave of a hand.

This time, I was left behind, while Achem went on to a mysterious destination.

I spent the next day on the river with a full boat. It pleased me to see it renewed by Achem's attentions. The seekers did not seem to notice.

Once ashore, I went directly up the bank to my abode. With all the attention given to the boat, I had not had the time the day before to finish attending to my obols, and I was eager to begin again.

I paused on the threshold. The air had been disturbed.

One long step, and I crossed to the storage tunnel. The door was locked, as always. Turning, I looked next to the corner where my work table stood.

Sure enough, my tools were scattered and my notebooks toppled. Some were flung open and discarded to the ground. Several obols had bounced and rolled across the tabletop.

I stood immobilized beside the destruction, rage choking my throat.

The case I'd left on my table was gone, along with the rows and rows of obols it contained.

And I knew just who had taken it.

Dusk had fallen, not with the setting of a sun but with a thickening of the dark. The banks kept a dim light that glowed from who knew where, and so I found Achem easily enough. They were seated with their back to a shelf of rock, legs stretched out. They examined a cloak in their lap.

At the sound of my approach, they looked up.

"Ah, you're back. Look, I retrieved my cloak. Never let it be said I'm not resourceful—"

"Give it back."

Achem's dark brows drew together. "Sorry? The cloak?"

I rose to my full height, so that I clouded the area around us. My shadow darkened this nothing corner and enveloped us. I made for Achem's throat, but this time they were faster.

They sprang from my reach. "Wait, now, wait! What's happened?"

"You know what happened. You spent all evening yesterday at my abode. Now I find a case is missing."

"*What* case?" Achem asked, now with the gall to sound exasperated.

"A case from my collection of obols. *Someone* has taken it."

"*I* didn't!" they protested.

I detected no falsehood in Achem's voice, but they did not speak with their usual confidence. A thread of guilt ran through their words.

I blinked from one space into existence in the next, so quickly Achem had no chance to escape. I slammed them into the stone wall and pinned them there by the neck. Achem's fingers pried at mine to no avail.

"Where is it?" My voice boomed.

This at last ended Achem's resistance. They made a noise of surrender.

I dropped them.

Achem crumpled to the ground, their legs giving out.

"Where is it?" I asked again.

Hand pressed to their throat, Achem managed. "I'm not sure. I did not take it. I only mentioned—" Achem winced with the strain of speaking through a bruised neck. "—they were saying you kept everything locked up behind an iron door. I just told one of them... I said it was possible the work station would have a half-full case on it. Enough riches for one person..."

"Why did you not go yourself?" I demanded. But I realized the trick now. Achem had hoped I would not be able to read any guilt in them, if they sent a proxy. "You sought to avoid blame."

Achem nodded stiffly. "She was desperate enough. It did not take much urging. I did not know she'd taken it already. She was supposed to come to me first. I only wanted one obol, as a payment for my tip."

"First?" I said. "Where are they going?"

A grim smile livened their pallid features. Then, they pointed upwards. "Where else is there to go?"

"The Upper World? Don't be ridiculous. What are they thinking, to go gambling one last time?"

A preposterous idea. While it was possible for a determined soul to make their way back up the path, the risk was great and the reward small. Even if they could find the way back to their homeland, upon reaching it they would realize how distant they had become from the living. They could not exist there for long, and eventually death would pull them back to the river.

Achem shrugged. Their voice rasped but was recovering. "Up there's the only option that makes any sense. What were they hoping to purchase down here? I've noticed a distinct lack of pottery..."

They would not be able to purchase anything in the Upper World either, not as incorporeal beings. But to a frightened soul, it would be the most logical option.

I straightened. Much as I wanted to punish Achem now, I could not afford to delay. "Stay here. I will return to deal with you."

"Hey, wait!" Achem, predictably, hustled to follow. "Are you sending hellhounds to drag them back?"

"No," I answered. A storm of anger still surged through my voice. "For this, I will go myself."

Achem followed like a puppy as I retrieved my pole and made for the path. I made no attempt to prevent them. Let them see the result of their poor choices.

The path was hardly a path at all, at first glance. Just a break in the cavern wall that could be mistaken for a cleft of rock. It was easy for the seekers to forget they had walked down here, and of their own volition. But if one followed the edge, the break became a gap. And then, in the space of a blink, we were on the path.

Achem whirled around, but the mists had closed in, and neither the banks nor the walls nor the river were visible any longer. That said, though we saw no other features, the path itself left no other option but forward. We walked its white curves and switchbacks side by side. I used the pole as a staff. My beard, white as the mist around us, swayed with each step.

We passed some others, seekers on their way down to the river. In their dreamlike state, they did not pay us any mind. Death washed the expressions from their faces and the individuality from their bodies. Most newly-deceased souls were docile. The path acted almost like a river itself, sweeping them downstream.

Some, of course, fought the current. Even those who arrived with obols wanted to return to the sunlit worlds, not realizing nothing waited for them there anymore. I rarely pursued these obstinate few. Eventually, they accepted the inevitable.

I charged along as fast as the path would allow. My thoughts raced on ahead of my feet. What if the thief had dropped the case? What if my obols had scattered irretrievably? My fingers tightened on my staff, knuckles whitening.

I wasn't sure yet how I would punish Achem and the other soul, but I had no doubt the answer would come to me. First though, I needed to secure my obols.

"Can I—" Achem attempted to speak once.

I rebuffed them with a glare, and their lips sealed shut. After that, they were occupied keeping up with me.

The path ended.

We came out into the Upper World on a cliffside. The sun blazed above us, warming the tan rocks and green shrubs. A warm breeze blew strongly from the sea —and what a view of it we had. From this vantage, the crystalline water stretched deep into the horizon, turning from a vibrant shade of turquoise to a jewel blue.

Achem laughed and turned their face to the sun. Their cloak slipped from their shoulders as they spread their arms. The sun brought out the warmth in their skin, and they almost looked like one of the living.

The thief, however, stuck out from the land in a swatch of darkness. They crouched a few yards away from us. Their clothing was ripped and faded, their hair wild, their eyes equally frantic. They seemed to have been stunned still by the reality of the Upper World and had not made it far from the path. In their grasping fingers, they clutched my case.

They did not try to run, and regardless, I was beside them in a moment.

"Thief," I said.

The seeker quailed. Their fingers loosed on the case and it landed in the dust.

"It was Achem's idea—!" the thief began their weak defense, but I interrupted.

"I do not need your guidance or your excuses!" Anger at the transgression still raged through me. I laid down the sentence that had taken form throughout our walk up. "You will not spend a hundred years on the shore," I intoned. "You will spend a thousand. Your body will fade and your mind with it, until you are as insubstantial as the mist. But first, I will tear you limb from limb."

I bore down, reaching for the mortal's throat.

"No, don't!"

I had forgotten about Achem. I ignored them and felt the satisfaction of my fingernails piercing the skin of the thief's neck.

"Charon, *don't!*" Achem shoved me back, sending the thief sprawling while I staggered. I was twice their height now and the assault did not affect me greatly, but my eyes narrowed.

"Move aside, Achem."

"No! It's my fault. Do not punish this person."

"I'll punish a thief in any way I see fit. Move aside!"

With this, I pushed them away. Achem stumbled as I passed by, reaching for the thief once more. I thought Achem would attack me again, but a moment too late I saw their arm flash downward, and then they had seized the case.

I lunged, but they skittered out of the way—right to the cliff's edge.

"No!" I cried, unnecessarily. Achem had stopped at the edge. The sun glittered on the waves far below.

"Do you really want a thief wandering your shores for a thousand years? Is that the only solution you can think of?"

"I have nothing to fear from a seeker," I snapped, my eyes never leaving my case. If they let their guard down for even a second, I would be on them.

"It would never have worked," Achem went on. "We cannot stay up here. She would have returned below. And I... it was my idea. Not hers."

"Come to your point."

"Show mercy. Let her cross the river."

I scoffed. "Let a thief cross the river? And one with no fare?"

Achem's gaze grew steely, and their countenance more serious than I'd ever seen before.

"Show mercy, or I throw this into the ocean." They hefted the case.

I snarled, "I have reached the end of my patience. Bring me my case. Bring what is owed to me!"

But my threat was empty. If they threw it, I would never be able to reclaim my lost treasures. Even if the case did not open and scatter its contents, the ocean would take it, and I could not leave my post for the years it would take to search. I tried a new approach. "The moment you step away from the cliff, I'll take it from you."

Achem shrugged. "Then I'll sit here while you deliver her." They inclined their head at the thief, who'd had the intelligence not to speak again.

I sighed. "I will only say I have done it, and you will have no proof."

"I know," said Achem, still in that voice of steel. "Which is why you must swear you'll do it. Swear on the Styx."

A wave of helpless fury flooded me. Such an oath would bind me blood and bone to my task. But there was nothing I could do. I cared more about my case than my revenge. Through gritted teeth, I said, "I swear."

The thief shook with fear as we walked the path. Perhaps they did not know I had never hurt a passenger, even when I was not oath-bound. A seeker without payment might meet my wrath, but a soul with passage booked fell under my protection. My charges were safe in my hands.

That said, I made no effort to allay their fears. My thoughts stewed on Achem. I hadn't thought I'd ever see them the way they looked on the cliff. So different from the smiling person who'd cleaned my boat. Their eyes had been wild with that familiar emotion: desperation. I'd been shocked to see it there, in someone who had acted so collected in the time I'd known them.

As we boarded the boat, I helped the thief as I'd helped all others in the millennia I'd done this work. Finally looking into their face, the arc of their life unfolded before me.

I'd expected to see desperation, but instead saw only a normal life. Their only sadness had been to die alone, with no one to place the obol. I did not like the thought that my world, the banks of the river, had changed them so utterly. How had they gone from the person I saw in their past life, to the faded soul now in front of me?

When I returned to collect Achem, they sat facing the ocean, watching the setting sun gild the waves.

"Now," I said, feeling no more indulgence.

Achem stood, straightened their shoulders, and handed my case to me. I breathed a sigh of relief.

They took one last lingering look at the sea and sky. Then we descended the path.

When we reached the banks, Achem had not softened. Nor had I.

"You will remain on the banks for a thousand years," I finally said, though the words came out flat and tired.

When Achem's face turned to mine, their mouth was set in a bitter twist. Seeing the lack of remorse there, my anger resurfaced.

"What right have you to resentment?" I snapped.

"I am sorry," they said.

My jaw clamped shut in surprise.

Achem continued stiffly, "I did not come to your abode meaning to find a way to rob you. It was... opportunistic, not nefarious. Hopefully you can understand why I had to try."

In their face, I saw grim acceptance, rather than the emotional contrition I had hoped for. My response was sharp. "You *had* to steal from me?"

Achem sighed deeply. In the slope of their shoulders, I saw I had made the wrong response. But what could I have said? Surely they had not expected me to forgive them, not after such an apology. I saw no justification for what they'd done. Was it my fault no one had placed the obol for them?

But before I could begin to correct Achem as to the error of their thinking, they turned their back on me and walked away.

Days passed. I did not see Achem. I spent my evenings in my abode. But my new obols piled up, and I had lost my taste for cataloguing. A strange feeling clung like spiderwebs to my psyche. I kept seeing Achem turning away from me. Kept feeling their disappointment.

I had to admit my own fault in the matter. Was it truly because of Achem that I had been too tired to properly store my obols? Or was it part of a trend? My own weariness—no, my apathy, increasing over the years—had caused me to slip.

I had thought all seekers to be desperate, grasping people. But the thief had not been that way in life. The banks of the river had made them that way. My river.

What would it make of Achem?

For some reason, I couldn't help but think of Joa. I could see the years of their friendship playing out across their lives. Before, my ability to see seekers' lives had felt like knowledge. I saw a few moments and thought I knew enough to cast judgment. But I had never asked how these moments strung together, or how each was a step toward change or growth. I had been incurious about the fullness of their lives.

Achem's actions had felt like betrayal to me because I had some illusion about our connection. But it was not their falsehood that had ruptured the bond. I had always been in a position of great power over their fate. I knew this, but the fact of it was so unexceptional to me I had not examined it. After all, I was only the ferryman. I had always thought seekers made their own choices, and the gods decided the rest.

Achem had faced 100 years of suffering. Small wonder they had sold out our burgeoning relationship for the chance at escape. Could I really lay the blame on the banks, the river, or the other souls?

I had made Achem desperate. And I did not like the way that realization sat with me. It meant I had made others desperate. It meant others had suffered unduly because of my apathy.

I traced memories, searching for an answer to my troubled mind. All I knew was that something must be made right.

In the end, I searched my shelves for the right case, and took out a cheap iron obol.

Achem sat wrapped in their cloak. They seemed to have acquired a knife as well. They had built a small fire in an alcove. With the wall on one side and the mists obscuring anyone else from sight, they had achieved a homey, intimate feel.

Sensing I might receive no invitation, I stepped up to the fire without one.

Achem grumbled at my presence, but without the malice they'd displayed at the clifftop.

I passed them the little coin. Surprise flitted across their face.

"You mean me to have this?"

I inclined my head. "It was Joa's obol."

Now Achem was truly shocked. They sat forward to examine the obol by the firelight.

"They are all valuable to me, you know. I care not whether they are gold or iron. All are precious."

Their fingers closed around it. "You are giving it to me?"

"Yes."

Achem bowed their head. Their eyes squeezed shut as emotion swept them. I waited for the shudders to pass.

When Achem lifted their head, I said, "I'd like to hear about Joa, in your own words."

Achem's thumb rubbed against the obol. "Why?"

"You are a person who can always find friends," I explained. "You must have had many. Why ask after this one?"

After a long pause, Achem said, "I liked who I was when I was with him."

"A rare gift," I said.

They spoke no more, and I chose not to press. I allowed Achem to spend a few minutes lost in their memories.

They changed the subject. "I want to stay and help the others on the bank."

Regretful, I shook my head. "You will lose yourself, seeker. Become a shade. You cannot help anyone that way. All must board my craft eventually. This is your time."

Achem leaned back against the cave wall. Firelight played over their features while they turned the obol over in their fingers.

"Why did you change your mind about me?" they asked.

I shifted my stance, and answered slowly. My thoughts were still swirling, unsettled, in my mind. "I thought there was a way of things. But now I see only a pattern of suffering, and myself just a link in a chain. I may yet break my own link."

For once Achem had no comment.
"Come when you are ready."

Some grow so used to the cold, hard existence on the banks they forget peace awaits them. Achem, who had felt the sun so recently, was not one. It took only a few days for them to arrive at my craft. Silently, I helped them in.

As we crossed, the gentle rocking of the boat cleansed the souls within. Soon the bank was shrouded by mist, and those aboard all but forgot the suffering they had experienced there. Achem's gaze met mine one last time as the sky lightened with new promise. Then their eyes turned toward the farther shore.

If you liked it, leave a comment. Authors love that!
Remember to subscribe to our e-mail updates so you'll know when new stories are posted.

About the story

The seed of this story began in the car with my friends, when someone made a joke about 'Charon the numismatist'. I loved the idea of the psychopomp treasuring his payment as more than just a toll. I immediately laid claim to the concept, since I was looking for topics for a short story writing challenge I wanted to do that summer.

Any writer can tell you that an exciting idea does not transform into a full story overnight. I let the concept percolate for a while, and finally sketched out the bones of the story in my plotting notebook. I outline my stories in a grid I created, basically a three-act structure that uses prompts focused on character choices and unintended consequences of those choices. This is how I developed Achem as an impact character for Charon. That summer (2021), I wrote six short stories over twelve days as a personal writing challenge. Though that may sound fast to some people, the purpose was not about speed but about creating variety while getting past any overthinking, sort of like NaNoWriMo. Each short story was distinct from the others in genre, tone, and character.

Taking on a well-known myth was something I had never done before. Hoping to strike a balance between honoring the original story and not boxing myself in, I did light research on Charon and the Greek underworld after the outline was written, but before writing the story. Luckily, myths often have multiple versions or interpretations, so I could work with what felt right for my story. Creating the original character of Achem also helped me to have an outlet not pre-structured by the existing stories.

The theme of death was another area that has been covered before by many an artist. However, like myths, there are many angles from which to talk about death. "The Numismatist" focuses on the pain and suffering of being alive, juxtaposed with the positive effect people can have on each other, even when they only have a short time together.

A question for the author

Q: When do you decide a story is finished?

A: For me, the first draft is about plot and the revisions are about character. I write epic fantasy, so my stories are usually plot-heavy and have a natural conclusion: the villain is defeated. But of course great stories are built around characters. For a story to be finished, I want to feel like I've done justice to each character's emotional arc. Are they in a different place from when they started? Does the reader understand the character well enough that their choices make sense? Do readers see a vision of what the future will look like for a character, even though the story is over? These questions are an important part of my revising process.

About the author

Cecelia Isaac is a fantasy author based in New Jersey. In her day job as a geospatial research specialist, she studies the decarbonization of the electrical grid. Her hobbies include being really bad at badminton. Besides fantasy, her favorite genre to read is mystery/thriller.

ceceliaisaac.com, @CeceliaIsaac

The Zoo Diaries

Frances Pauli

Part Two

Previously…

We met the animals incarcerated in the Rainriver Zoological Gardens, a public animal experience. The zoo is struggling financially to meet the needs and requirements of its inhabitants who in turn struggle with the reality of life in captivity. Here the Sulcata tortoise longs for his missing cage-mate. The hyena pines for her lost cubs, and the macaque monkey struggles with his coffee addiction. Free from the bars which restrict the others, a wicked crow taunts them in their misery. Meanwhile, budget cuts forced the zoo to change all predators to commercial diet in lieu of raw meat.

Desperate to find Miranda, the tortoise, Oliver, escaped his enclosure. His tunnel led him to the elephant, Shanti, who assisted in getting him outside of the fences and into freedom. The escape spawned a flurry of gossip, led by the crow, who used the news to taunt the other animals. More significantly, the zoo-cam video feed caught Oliver and Shanti's interaction, sparking renewed public interest in the zoo.

Zoo Admissions

The gates are choked with visitors the morning after the video goes viral. Admission sales break the all-time zoo record, and the staff struggles to keep the lines moving. Counting is not standard procedure, as they have never approached maximum capacity before. The recent financial difficulties make it unwise to turn anyone away, however.

Someone calls a manager, who is delighted to pass on the news to the Board. More hours are requested, more staff required, but all decisions will be left to the next meeting. It could easily be a fluke, and the bottom line does not allow for any margin of error.

Elephant Paddock

Shanti counts 300 peanuts, and the day isn't even half over. She counts them twice, eying the crowd at the rail suspiciously. It is too many. There is no mathematical explanation for a 200 percent increase. More than that, she decides—they are still arriving with their cameras and their bags of nuts.

They cheer and shout to her.

Shanti rearranges the peanuts, sighs, and goes back to lining up straw. She divides yesterday's nuts by three, multiplies today's haul, and considers the increase. Something out of the ordinary is happening.

Numbers, she knows, do not lie. They do, sometimes, seem to carry a big stick, a stick that can knock and jab until you are forced to comply with them.

As if her thought summons them, They-who-sweep and They-who-bring-food arrive. *Their* sticks hang from their waists, and she admits that they are slow to use them. When they do, the prods and thumps are easy enough to bear.

Shanti obeys them without error. She remembers the circus.

Today they keep their sticks dangling. He-who-sweeps carries a broom. She-who-brings-food fills Shanti's manger with fresh hay. At the railing, the voices lift and turn as one to questions. Someone waves a fluffy, stuffed effigy of a turtle.

Shanti blinks at it. She wonders if they have caught Oliver yet, if her crime has somehow brought the crowd, and if it has, whether or not she will face punishment. Her trunk lowers, swings. She watches the sticks and barely notices when He-who-sweeps erases her calculations with a deft swipe of the broom.

Beside the railing, the crowd surges and shouts. The phony turtle dances. She-who-brings-food seems calm. She leans against the rail, chats with the others.

Shanti relaxes.

She will not be punished. She turns back to her peanuts as another shower of shells lands.

There are too many.

The Crow

Debra finds her murder in the elephant paddock. They have surrounded the huge, gray animal and are swiping peanuts the crowd throws to her.

The elephant uses her trunk to gather as many of the nuts into a pile as possible. She pivots, brushes the ground, and the braver crows duck in and steal from her pile.

Debra isn't hungry. She has filled up on popcorn and is still feeling dizzy from too much latte. The sport appeals to her, however. She is faster than many of the others. She could slip right past the rubbery trunk.

First, she lands on a rock just inside the paddock rail. There are too many visitors today. The zoo paths are choked with bodies, but the densest mass grows like a tumor around the elephant paddock.

Debra quickly decides the two are somehow related. She knows They-who-keep-prisoners are searching for the tortoise, but if these others are here to assist, they are stupid. The fugitive has long since left this area.

Debra flaps and caws at them. Idiots. There is clearly no sign of the tortoise here. His tunnel emerges in the center of the paddock, and Debra flies to the dry opening to investigate. The hole is empty, as she imagined. A line of scraped tracks leads from the tunnel toward the elephant's shelter.

Debra follows them, snatching a peanut as she passes the fray and earning a chorus of cheers from her cohort.

The murder shuffles, becomes bolder. They rush the peanuts three at a time, and the elephant lands a blow, swings her trunk, and sends one black body fluttering, stunned and bruised, across the packed ground.

Debra chuckles and struts. She explores the shelter and finds nothing but spent straw. She flies up, landing on the mounted black eye of the camera and presses her head against it. It is shiny and cool, and she pecks twice at the lens before flying off.

The tracks continue to the corner where the escape occurred, just as Debra knew they would. If They-who-keep-prisoners know the elephant helped, perhaps they are watching her, guarding her, until she can be properly punished.

Debra thinks she would like to witness that too. She thinks she should linger here, but she also sees the macaque huddling against his bars. She sees him, and her breath still reeks of coffee, still carries enough of his bean to drive him into a frenzy.

She leaves the paddock behind. They won't punish the elephant while the crowds are here, and she has an ape to torture.

Wolf Run

The wolf pack is led by a pale gray male and his mate. She is black from nose to tail tip, and her two pups look exactly like her. They are ten weeks old today, and neither of them pays any heed to their mother's rules regarding pigeons.

This morning, three plump, gray birds have entered pack territory. They waddle across the short, border grass while the adult wolves are occupied with the minced meat that has been tossed into the enclosure.

The pups' bellies are round and full of milk. They wrestle in the grass where the birds can clearly see them, and when the pigeons do not fly away in fear, the game shifts to one of stalking and hunting.

They crouch, tongues lolling freely, and watch the gray heads bob, the fat bodies move, one slow step at a time. They ease closer. Their haunches are tense for springing and chasing. Their hearts beat an excited music in their flattened ears.

"I wouldn't do that," the fattest pigeon speaks.

"It's rude," another coos. "Not friendly at all."

The pups sit up. Mother has taught them of rudeness, but they'd never guessed it applied to pigeons.

"We're hunting you," the bolder pup announces.

"Rude," the birds coo all together, suddenly huddled into a much larger mass of feathers. "Roo-oo-ood."

"If you hunt us," the fattest once again takes control of the conversation, "then we'll never tell you about it."

"About what?" the more curious pup asks while the bold one lifts a rear paw, absently scratching behind one ear.

"About the news, silly," the pigeon says. "About freedom."

"What's freedom?" the curious pup asks.

His sister whispers into his ear, "Mom said pigeons are liars."

"I think she meant crows." The pigeon, having heard the insult, puffs up considerably. "Crows lie. Pigeons always tell the truth."

Neither pup can imagine anyone *always* telling the truth. They exchange a look that says as much, deciding as one that Mother has been right all along. As usual.

"It's beside the point," the bird snaps. "Someone has gotten free, you see."

"What is free?" the wolf pups sing together.

"Free is when you can go anywhere you like," the bird explains. "Free is going outside, doing whatever you want."

"We already have that," the pups scoff, giggle, and make ready to bound away again.

Pigeons, it turns out, are boring.

"You don't, you know," the pigeon says. "Not really."

"Do too."

"Don't."

"We do whatever we want all day long," the brave pup cries.

"We go all over," her brother adds. "I even went to the rock on top of the den once."

"Liar," his sister barks. "When?"

"But you can't go over there." The pigeon turns, stupidly showing them his back, and faces the high wall, the rock-that-cannot-be-climbed. "Could you go over there if you wanted? Can you leave this cage?"

The wolves, who have been considering pouncing on him, freeze and stare up at the barrier. They have never considered anything else might *be* out there, and it gives them an uncomfortable fluttering feeling in their full bellies to think on it.

"We could," the bold pup says. "We just don't want to."

"Freedom," the pigeon coos. "Now you know. Freedom is what's *outside*. It's what you can't have *inside*."

The pups stare at the high wall. The birds, certain their point has been made at last, take to wing, fly up, one after the other, over the top of the wall that is too high to climb.

The curious pup whimpers.

His sister growls softly.

"You know," she says. "I think Mother was right about pigeons."

Her brother lies down, rests his head on his paws and watches the wall.

Mother is always right.

Ape House

Gonzo throws a turd at the crow. He knows better, knows it only debases him, that the crow will laugh harder for it. That it will rile up the other macaques until their flinging becomes a ruckus and the path outside is streaked in feces.

He cannot help himself. The devil-bird reeks of bean. She teases him with her breath, flapping her wings to waft the sweet aroma through the bars.

His turd nearly hits her.

The crow shrieks and launches into the air. Her mockery echoes in her wake, stays with him long after she has moved on to her next victim.

Gonzo's cagemates scree and fling their turds through the bars. They leap and chatter, taking up the game with zealous ferocity.

Gonzo burns with shame. He slinks to the little square door and hides in the shadow of the rope vines. She-who-sweeps will not appreciate the mess he's inspired. She may throw stones at them if no one is looking.

They are easy enough to dodge, usually ping off the bars anyway, but her anger makes him feel small and shivery.

It is the crow's fault, his shame.

It is the bean's fault.

Gonzo wishes for his home forest. He imagines sneaking from the trees, raiding the plantation for fistfuls of the sweet red coffee cherries. He salivates, grinds his teeth together. The cherries hold the bean, and the bean holds ecstasy.

The others tire of flinging and take to the ropes. Gonzo watches their shadows dance over the cage floor. He imagines his wild troop swinging through the branches. He imagines moist air and an entire jungle full of life, where the song of birds is never silent, and their voices cry of useful things: food, danger, mating.

There were no crows in his jungle. Only here, where madness lives, do the devils fly on jet black wings, their voices tasting of his bean and their words begging for murder.

MEMO

RAINRIVER ZOOLOGICAL GARDENS

TO All EMPLOYEES

IT HAS COME TO OUR ATTENTION THAT ZOOCAM FOOTAGE HAS BEEN UPLOADED TO A THIRD-PARTY SITE BY ONE OF OUR STAFF MEMBERS WITHOUT THE PERMISSION OF MANAGEMENT.

ALL EMPLOYEES ARE REQUIRED TO SIGN A NON-DISCLOSURE OF COMPANY PROPERTY AND POLICIES AGREEMENT UPON HIRING. IF YOU NEED TO RE-READ THIS DOCUMENT, COPIES CAN BE FOUND IN HUMAN RESOURCES.

AS FOR THE PERSON OR PERSONS RESPONSIBLE FOR HACKING THE ZOO WEBSITE AND POSTING THE "BEST OF RAINRIVER" COMPILATION, WE IMPLORE YOU TO COME FORWARD BY

CONTACTING DR. WHEELER IN THE ZOO'S PUBLICITY OFFICE.

AT THIS TIME, WE CAN PROMISE NO REPERCUSSION OR RETRIBUTIVE ACTION WILL BE TAKEN.
—ZOO MANAGEMENT

Lion Enclosure

Charlie paces the long grass beside his trench. Above him, the morsels clog the railings, choking out the sky and jostling for a better view of him.

He has been fed minced meat this morning, and his instincts shy away from the unnatural, pre-chopped meal. His belly is full, but he is restless, unhappy.

At the rail, they wave and flash. There are too many up there, and the cameras fire non-stop. Their arms juggle snacks, purses, latte cups, and the always-aromatic hot dogs sleeping in their paper boats.

The burr of electronic shutters clicking becomes a swarm of insects. The urgency of the crowd swells as their cameras compete for the lion's attention. Someone bumps hard against the railing, pushed from behind and nearly toppling forward into a fateful plunge.

Their paper boat capsizes, and Charlie watches, suddenly still, suddenly the perfect subject, as a fat, fleshy hot dog somersaults into the trench.

He hears it land, hears the wet impact and opens his mouth, huffing in the meat scent that has infringed upon his territory but lies now just beyond the wire-that-bites.

It will drive him mad, that smell. It will linger in his memory for days while he digests the mince. While he rolls in the dung of distant zebras. Charlie eyes the wire, considers.

A small black body rockets into the trench. More follow, feathered bullets aimed directly at his sanity.

The crows scrap over the fallen meat. They caw and flutter. They tear the hot dog into bits, and Charlie hears it squeak, hears the flesh give to their claws and beaks.

He dares a step toward the wire, but the birds are off already. One by one, they vacate the trench, taking his instincts in their bony claws, and carrying them away.

Hyena Pen

Alice's cage is three paces by four. She can leap to the second highest step on her rock in a single bound. On a slow day, the faces at her bars make her cringe and pant.

Today, the crowd blots out the bushes. She cannot see across the narrow paths, cannot see anything aside from the rows of shiny eyes and bared teeth.

When she carried her pups, They-who-sweep-her-shit hung dark cloth around the bars of her enclosure. They posted signs requesting quiet that were only ignored by the least sensitive of zoo patrons.

She wishes for those curtains today, closes her eyes and pants from the top of her rock. She wishes it were twice as high, wishes she could run for more than three by four paces.

Her sides heave. She ignores the massive knuckle bone she's been working at throughout the night. She is crowded. Anxious.

She thinks of the strange rock and his quest for the aviary. It *is* the second path, isn't it? She can't remember where that knowledge came from now, if it is something she overheard or only something imagined. Couldn't it just as easily be the first path… or the last?

Alice shivers and turns her body slowly so that she faces the wall. She tucks her tail against her legs, curls and hides her spotted head beneath her paws.

She is still. She is silent. She imagines she is an ordinary stone, holding her breath for longer and longer periods.

She has lived in the zoo her entire life, and she knows more than one trick. They-who-watch are easily bored. They do not linger over nothing. They do not come to the zoo to stare at stones.

Grizzly Grotto

Hector's artist has taken her book and gone. His railing is a solid wall of expectant faces, and he considers lumbering to the square door and hiding in his den, but They-who-bring-food have hidden chunks of frozen fruit inside his stump, and the sweet smell calls to him.

His nose turns toward the odor, wandering as if it seeks to leave his muzzle behind. He sits, reaches with both front paws, and sinks his sickle claws into the soft wood.

Already, it bears the hieroglyphics of his attention. His marks cross and re-cross up and down the short tower.

The food waits in a hollow at the top of the stump, but the game must be played first. If only for appearances.

Hector claws and tears, lips rippling, and he imagines that someone, somewhere claps and cheers. Once he's made a show of searching, he roots into the hidden space, uses his tongue to remove a cold, hard strawberry, and sucks on it.

At the railing, a dozen shutters click. They aim their phones and their cameras in his direction and try to capture his likeness.

Philistines.

Hector offers them his rump, continues to eat the fruit secretively, covetously. He snorts and rumbles, licks his black lips.

He has only one artist, and *she* would never stoop to photography.

Tortoise Abroad

Oliver waits until the pathways are vacant. He hides between a trio of garbage cans and an overgrown rhododendron. He has eaten grass all day, quietly munching in a narrow circle while They-who-come-to-stare enjoy the zoo.

He thinks it must be a special holiday, for the crowd is thick, and the noise of their steps and voices deafening. After the gates close, it takes twice as long to clean the zoo, and some of the trash is simply left to skitter down the lanes and into the bushes.

At dusk, They-who-sweep-and-bring-food-and-clean-poop rush up and down the paths. They shine hand-held lights into corners and crevices. Oliver knows they are looking for him, but this is not his first zoo, nor is it his first escape.

He waits until the walks have been silent for a long time before creeping out into the open.

"There you are," a stupid pigeon nearly stops his heart.

Oliver ignores the bird and eases back to the nearby path, the second path, the one that will lead him to Miranda.

At least it's not a crow.

"Everyone is looking for you," the pigeon says. It has hopped down from one of the trash cans and now it bounces along at his side. "The zoo's gone mad with it."

"Let it," Oliver says, heaving his great shell forward, "go mad."

"Everyone's talking about you."

Oliver reaches the edge where the grass meets asphalt. He will make less obvious tracks on the latter but will also be more exposed following it.

"Are they still looking?" He knows better than to engage with gossips, but the rotten pigeons always seem to have a broader view of the world.

"No." Taking his questions as friendship, the pigeon flaps its wings, hops up, and settles itself on top of Oliver's shell. "Everyone gave up hours ago."

Oliver thinks it hasn't been that long. He believes, had he been a fiercer creature, that the pigeon would be dead.

Its claws tickle his dome, but he is not flexible, not fast enough to dislodge it.

"Where are we going?" it asks.

"Aviary," Oliver huffs and steps out onto the asphalt. "This way."

"The aviary isn't this way," the pigeon says. "Whatever gave you that idea?"

Oliver pauses. He stares down the path and thinks of Miranda, of the hyena who had surely never left her cage. Whose mind has been twisted by her life in a box.

"Where?" he asks.

"I can show you," the pigeon says. "They'll never believe it, never live it down, if I do it."

"Where?" Oliver repeats. His limbs are cold already, and the night caresses his shell with fingers of ice. Only the spot where the bird rests is warm, and he chooses to take that as a sign. "Guide me."

"You bet I will," the pigeon says. "The crows will *never* live it down."

Oliver sighs. He wonders if the hyena wasn't right. But when the pigeon flaps and shifts against his shell, when it coos, "This way," Oliver sets off, obediently, in a whole new direction.

The Crow

Debra circles the park above the high fences and the short trees. She watches the search eagerly, her excitement lessened only slightly by the fact that They-who-search do not carry weapons.

There is too much chaos to be disappointed, too much action in a world that lives by routine, by feeding schedules, business hours, and state-mandated rules and regulations. There is trash lingering in the walks. There is a broken fence in the petting zoo where the weight of the crowd proved too much for the poorly maintained wood.

Debra watches until the search ends, then she circles on her own. Her murder has settled for the night, tucked into the branches of the tallest tree near the elephant paddock.

There is no point in lingering there. The tortoise has roamed far during the previous night. Debra has seen traces of him, followed bits and scraps of tracks from the African Savannah halfway across the zoo.

She flies over the cat house now, and she knows he will move again soon. He is clever, almost crow clever, and he's been waiting somewhere for the paths to clear. She lands atop the cat house roof, hops down its length, and gazes out to where the deep pit trenches of the bear enclosures wait.

The zoo falls quiet. Everything sleeps, still as usual, ordinary as any other night. Except for the hyena. Debra thinks the hyena should be crying, curled up on her rock and whimpering to herself in her grating, feather-lifting voice.

And she is not.

Tonight, the free-standing block that houses the weird beast, that sandwiches her forever between the bears and the house of true cats, is silent. It is a very loud sound, that quiet. A heavy absence.

Debra dives from the roof, sweeps over grass and paths alike, and lands in a bush in front of the grieving hyena's home. She expects to find the animal asleep, her sobbing spent at last. Instead, she sees the spotted body pacing near the front bars. Too quiet. Too quick. First one way and then the other.

"Hello," Debra calls.

"Stone?"

Interesting. Debra considers before answering, finds words that are open and as slippery as a wet vine.

"Perhaps." She hunkers deeper into the foliage, hides her body, and softens her voice. "Perhaps not."

"It's not the second path," the hyena blurts. "I told him it was, but now I'm not certain."

"You told him?" Debra's plumage prickles. "Did you?"

"I told him." The hyena turns, trots to the far corner then pivots and skims right back. "He's looking in the wrong place. I just know it."

"Looking for..." Debra lets the word stretch into a compulsion.

"The aviary," the hyena replies. "Looking for a bird, and all birds are in the aviary."

This is not, in fact, true, but what would a hyena know of it?

"I see." Debra shifts her feet and the branches crackle.

They hyena freezes, head up, ears swiveling. "Who are you?"

Debra tries to think of a slippery answer, but she has spotted the Sulcata's tracks in the grass below and the excitement of this evidence dulls her tongue.

"Are you the stone's mother?" Something in the tone of that provides the right answer.

"Yes," Debra lies, sure now that she knows what 'stone' they speak of.

"He took the second path," they hyena repeats. "But I'm not sure it's right. I'm not sure he'll find her there."

"Find who?" Debra risks a direct question.

"The bird who used to live with him," the hyena offers freely.

It is too delightful, too awful to bear in silence and Debra cackles.

The hyena growls, lowers and bristles all down her back. "Who are you?" she demands, suspicions lacing through her words. It is too much. Too perfect.

It is bound to end in disaster.

And Debra has already flown away.

Elephant Paddock

There are even more visitors than yesterday, an impossible number of faces packed into a living wall around Shanti's pen.

The peanuts are beginning to irritate her.

She steps through a sea of shells, crunching, swinging her trunk through the piles while another shower makes it all impossible to count.

Around Oliver's tunnel, the demon birds have gathered. Shanti tries ignoring the crowd, tries counting the birds instead. One rotten crow. Two awful, obnoxious crows. Three...

"It's all because of you," one of the murder caws.

"You let him out," another shouts.

"You'll be punished."

"They're all here to watch."

"Punishment." They take that up like a chant. "Punish, punish, punishment."

Shanti thinks they're liars. It's been three days, three long nights since the tortoise erupted inside her paddock. Three since she lifted the fence, and the sticks have not struck. She is not punished, and she thinks she will not be.

Four lying devil crows. Five…

She did help Oliver escape, and she does wonder where he's gone with his domed shell and its thirteen perfect hexagonal tiles with twenty-four partials around the edges. Shanti enjoyed counting him. She hopes he has found his bird, but she wonders if he might wander back in this direction afterwards.

If he does, she will lift the fence for him. She will guard his tunnel for his return, and maybe he will let her count him all over again.

"Punishment." The crows screech.

Shanti swings her trunk and charges them.

"Shit."

"Crazy."

"Mad, mad!"

They scatter, cursing her, singing epithets.

Shanti counts their shadows as they fly. Six fat, furious silhouettes. Six sides to each hexagon.

She stands over an empty tunnel and waits for the tortoise to return.

ZOO FLIER

WIN CASH!!!

ANNOUNCING THE FIRST EVER
RAINRIVER ZOOLOGICAL GARDEN
VIDEO CONTEST
"COME TO THE ZOO AND CAPTURE THE
MAGIC"

$3,000 IN CASH PRIZES*
1ST PLACE: $1500
RUNNER-UP VIDEO: $1000
BEST STILL PHOTOGRAPH: $500

SEE YOU AT THE ZOO!

*PRIZE MAY BE PAID IN ZOO BUCKS AT WINNER'S DISCRETION

The Board declares the viral video to be an unprecedented opportunity. The chaos at the gates seems quite sufferable once the daily admissions are tallied and profits totaled. Another lane is added, another booth opened, and talk shifts to the idea of promoting the contest.

Someone suggests contacting the local radio station.

Maintenance complains about the additional work, and one of the zoo veterinarians brings up stress and animal welfare. Both topics are tabled until the next meeting.

The contest goes forward as planned.

Ape House

Gonzo sits in shadow while his troop dances for the crowd. His headache is not lessened by the steady clicking of camera shutters. Nor is it any better for the constant screeching and hooting of the other macaques.

They swing from one rope to the next. They race up, around, and over, tumbling and wrestling while the cameras fight over the best angle.

Gonzo has tried to go back inside, but the little square door is blocked. He is shut out. He is on display. It is his own fault.

Earlier, They-who-bring-food left one of their paper vessels too close to the cage bars. There had been three of them that morning, two carrying tubs of sliced fruit and chopped vegetables, and a third bringing them each a vessel of the hot, steaming, bean juice favored by They-who-sweep-and-bring-food-and-clean-feces.

The tubs were set in the center aisle, between the rows of ape house cages, and the drinks evenly distributed.

Gonzo watched the dance of vessels. He pressed his nose against cool bars and let his gaze drift from one end of the aisle to the next, following the bean.

The tubs were hauled to each cage door. The food was distributed, and every free, hairless paw waved a vessel, wafting steam and aroma from cage to cage. When the tub reached the macaque enclosure, it was heaved up onto the cage floor. The-one-who-manned-the-door passed their vessel to The-one-who-watched-for-escape, whose paw already lifted their own drink to pink lips. With a shrug, they took the second and set it down beside Gonzo's cage.

And he was on it.

Gonzo leapt sideways along the bars, stuffing both arms through to his armpits. His fingers scrambled for the vessel, met with smooth hot paper, snatched, and lifted.

They-who-bring-food made a noise of challenge, a barking, choking sound that brought Gonzo's teeth out, that peeled back his lips in defiance.

The vessel was batted out of his grip. Suddenly, it was tumbling, spraying hot liquid in a wasted swath across the aisle. The vessel hit the concrete with a hollow thunk. Gonzo shrieked and stretched for it, catching a single drop of spray in his paws. He drew his fingers in, stuffed them into his mouth, and sucked.

The taste was so brief, so muted that he might have imagined it. His fingers were burned.

They-who-bring-food shouted at one another, waving their arms at the aisle, the cage, at Gonzo.

He screeched and lunged at the bars, pressing the keepers two steps further into the aisle. He showed his fangs, howled, and slammed his fists against the cage floor. His troop fell upon the food, but Gonzo ignored them, continued to rail.

When the others finished, wandering out into the sunshine, he sulked, hunkered inside until a long broom pushed through the bars, pushed, and harried him until he followed the troop.

Then the door was blocked. The flat, unbreakable panel slid into place, and Gonzo was left to face the outside world, the constant flutter of the cameras, the troops frenzy.

He sits, in the rope shadows, and he stuffs his sore fingers into his mouth, sucks at them as if he can taste anything at all.

Lion Enclosure

Charlie tries to ignore the morsels, but they are pounding on the clear, den wall. He lies against the barrier, back to the crowd and mouth hanging open, drinking in the scents that reach him only faintly.

From the railing, the meaty, tangy snack odors call like half-forgotten dreams, just out of reach.

Charlie's belly is full of the tasteless minced meat. His ears twitch in time to the morsels' pounding. Each impact of a tiny fist a hard finger against his spine. He narrows his gaze, blinks at the sunlight outside the den, where the lionesses lounge for the crowd at the railings.

They are basking in the attention, in the eyes of a crowd unlike any Charlie can remember in his life at the zoo.

A tap-tapping at the glass drags his head around. It is sharper, more insistent than the idle thumps, and when he looks, a round face has pressed into a pancake grimace right beside his own.

Charlie yawns, stretching his jaws wide enough to swallow the morsel's whole head.

"I see you, morsel," that yawn says. "I taste you there."

The morsel squeals. It is a muffled sound, filtered through the barrier, but Charlie loves it. He curls his tongue and heaves to all fours, facing the tiny morsel and huffing a warning.

Both of the small one's fists press in beside his face, smoosh against the barrier and pale, flatten.

Charlie bats one paw out, pats at the smooth surface until the morsel shrieks and moves. It doesn't run. Instead, it dances up and down, batting its own paws together before pressing up against the clear wall again.

Charlie imagines it tastes like the squeaky meat sticks. He lets his tongue reach out and licks the barrier, runs his mouth over and over the morsel while, behind it, the tall ones clap and wave.

Hyena Removed

Alice wakes in unfamiliar surroundings. Three of the walls are solid, and through the short stretch of bars she can see a narrow aisle and another cage across from hers.

The stair-step rock is missing. There is a thin shelf along one wall, but it is too narrow, too insubstantial for lounging.

She ponders it and remembers vaguely that she knows this from experience.

Alice sniffs, wrinkling her muzzle. Her head is fuzzy inside as well as out. She remembers eating in the evening, an entire bowl of meaty, strange-smelling mince. She remembers struggling to climb the stair-step rock and slipping, falling asleep instead in the straw at its base.

Now she is *inside*. There is no chattering crowd, but there is also no sun, no sky at all to tell her if it's day or night.

There are lights, but they are weirdly too dim and too bright simultaneously. Impossible to look at. Pale enough to only illuminate half the cage. Across the aisle, a sleek shape moves in its own enclosure. It is low and lanky, some sort of spotted feline. Alice remembers she's seen it before.

She has been *here* before.

Alice pants. She flicks her tail and rises, shakily, on her four paws. She begins to inspect the cage. Her nose presses into each corner, every crevice. It finds no hint of her own scent, but she is certain, by the time she finishes, that she has spent time here before.

Her paws remember how many paces fit along each wall. They track a familiar path around the space, easily, automatically.

Alice sits, stares at the shadow cat, and tries to think. It was before her pups but not *long* before.

That time, she tried the ledge and fell. That time she burned with her estrus, paced and paced until they finally released her back into her cage to find...

Alice relaxes. She believes this is temporary. She remembers, and as if on command, her body slumps. Her paws stretch, forward and back, and she rolls onto her side. Tired. Calm.

She closes her eyes and waits.

If you liked it, leave a comment. Authors love that!
Remember to subscribe to our e-mail updates so you'll know when new stories are posted.

Copyright

Title information

Metaphorosis February 2023

ISSN: 2573-136X (online)
ISBN: 978-1-64076-251-0 (e-book)
ISBN: 978-1-64076-252-7 (paperback)

Copyright

Works of fiction

This book contains works of fiction. Characters, dialogue, places, organizations, incidents, and events portrayed in the works are fictional and are products of the author's imagination or used fictitiously. Any resemblance to

Publisher

Metaphorosis
a magazine of speculative fiction

Metaphorosis Magazine is an imprint of Metaphorosis Publishing
Neskowin, OR, USA

www.metaphorosis.com

Discounts available

Substantial discounts are available for educational institutions, including writing workshops. Discounts are also available for quantity purchases. For details, contact Metaphorosis at metaphorosis.com/about

Metaphorosis Publishing

Metaphorosis offers beautifully written science fiction and fantasy. Our imprints include:

Metaphorosis Magazine
Plant Based Press
Verdage
Vestige

You can also find us:
@MetaphorosisMag, @Metaphorosis
www.facebook.com/metaphorosis

Help keep Metaphorosis running by supporting us at
Patreon.com/metaphorosis

See more about some of our books on the following pages.

Metaphorosis Magazine

Metaphorosis
a magazine of speculative fiction

Metaphorosis is an online speculative fiction magazine dedicated to quality writing. We publish an original story every week, along with author bios, interviews, and notes on story origins.

We also publish monthly print and e-book issues, as well as yearly Best of and Complete anthologies.

Come and see us online at magazine.Metaphorosis.com.

Metaphorosis
Best of 2016
Metaphorosis
2016
Editor
B. Morris Allen

Plant Based Press

Vegan-friendly science fiction and fantasy, including anthologies of the year's best SFF stories, from 2016-2020.

Chambers of the Heart

speculative stories
by
B. Morris Allen

A heart that's a building, a dog that's a program, a woman sinking irretrievably — stories about love, loss, and motion.

Susurrus

A darkly romantic story of magic, love, and suffering.

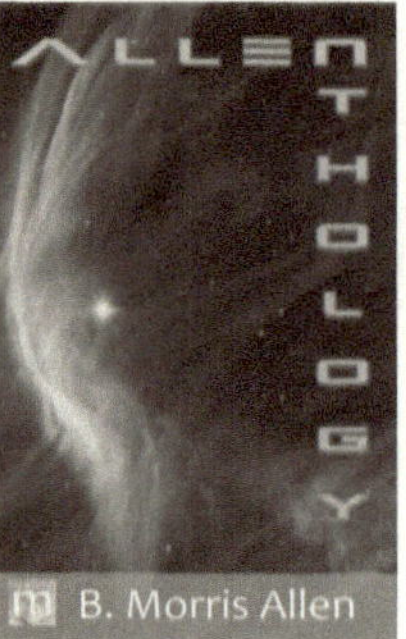

Allenthology: Volume I

Including three full collections of SFF stories.

Reading 5X5 x2

Duets

How do authors' voices change when they collaborate?

A round-robin of five talented science fiction and fantasy authors collaborating with each other and writing solo.

Including stories by Evan Marcroft, David Gallay, J. Tynan Burke, L'Erin Ogle, and Douglas Anstruther.

Score

an SFF symphony

An anthology with an emotional score from the heights of joy to the depths of despair – but always with a little hope shining through.

Reading 5X5

Five stories, five times

See how different writers take on the same material.

Reading 5X5

Writers' Edition

Two extra stories, the story seed, and authors' notes on writing.

Vestige

Novelettes, novellas, and novels by Metaphorosis authors.

The Nocturnals
Mariah Montoya

Night is Dangerous. Day is deadly.

Where day and night last thirty years, humans move constantly stay ahead of the night and cruel Nocturnals that call it home. But a boy is lost out there.